ISBN: 978-1-7645666-0-5

Author's Note

"Conversations with Famous Figures" is a series of fictitious interview style conversations conducted between Jeremy Francis Sams and some of the most fascinating figures in history, including Einstein, Shakespeare, and Caesar. There is also a special conversation with God to launch the series. The conversations tell their captivating stories by drawing out and delving into the deepest and most sensitive aspects of the figures' lives, exposing information never revealed before or presenting the known facts in a totally fresh light. The dialogue, as well as being erudite, is often playful and humorous, leaving the reader both educated and entertained.

"You think death ends a legacy? I conquered that too."

— Julius Caesar

"Time is relative. So is truth. Ask better questions."

— Albert Einstein

"All the world's a stage, but the dead have the best lines."

— William Shakespeare

"Ask not what history can tell you—ask who's still willing to talk."

— John F. Kennedy

"They breached my walls, but not my will. Even in ruin, an empire speaks."

— Constantine XI Palaiologos

"I gave them free will. You gave them microphones."

— God

Disclaimer

This is a work of fiction, specifically alternate history. While it incorporates real historical figures such as John F. Kennedy and Albert Einstein, and references actual events, the narrative, characterizations, and dialogues are fictionalized and speculative.

The inclusion of historical facts is intended to provide context and authenticity to the story, but the interpretations, motivations, and personal details attributed to real individuals are products of the author's imagination. These portrayals are not intended to represent actual beliefs, behaviours, or actions of the individuals depicted.

This work is not intended to defame, malign, or harm any person, living or deceased, or any organization. It is a creative exploration of historical possibilities and should be read as a fictional reimagining rather than a factual account.

CONTENTS

A Conversation With God 1

A Conversation With Gaius Julius Caesar 14

A Conversation With Constantine XI Dragas Paleologos, The Last of the Romans 38

A conversation With Albert Einstein 59

A Conversation With William Shakespeare 83

A Conversation With Leonardo Da Vinci 110

A Conversation With John Fitzgerald Kennedy, 35th President of the United States 134

Glossary 164

A CONVERSATION WITH GOD

'So, why did you do it?' I ask.

'I was bored,' God replies casually, looking at his fingernails.

'You were bored. I see.' Not quite the response I was expecting.

'Well, and I was curious, I guess,' God adds as an afterthought.

'Curious. How so?' I ask, somewhat puzzled.

'Curious in the same way a scientist is curious; curious to experiment, to test theorems and so on,' he states in a matter-of-fact way.

'So, this is all an experiment, driven out of boredom and curiosity?'

'That's about the sum of it.' God shrugs – I almost detect a hint of embarrassment as he looks away and stares at the wall.

'I see.' This conversation is not going the way I expected. 'Let me take you back to the creation, if I may.'

'Okay,' God shrugs with obvious nonchalance. 'But she didn't do it,' he quickly adds, almost defensively.

'Didn't do what?'

'Eat the forbidden fruit.'

'You mean Eve?'

'Yes. Well, yes and no. She ate the apple, but only because she was hungry. I hadn't forbidden it. I hadn't forbidden the eating of apples, so in that sense, she didn't do it. In fact, it was a pretty harsh winter that year. Not much to go around, so she reached out for a Washington Red hanging there on the tree. Why not? I mean, I would – I like apples.'

'A Washington Red?' I ask, somewhat perplexed at this level of detail.

'Yup,' he replies. very matter-of-factly.

'But why a Washington Red? Why not a Granny Smith, or a Fuji, or a Golden Delicious?' This conversation is taking a surreal, even somewhat farcical, turn. Apples!

'Soil and climatic conditions were the deciding factors, I guess,' God states indifferently.

'But the Garden of Eden *is* the garden of plenty, is it not?'

'Nope. Not really. That was all you guys. Medieval propaganda. A narrative to suit the Church. All part of rationalizing the irrational. A convenient figment, upon which many other convenient figments were built. I don't think they could really reconcile the fact that I was omnipotent and all merciful yet, would tolerate pestilence, and plague, and so on. So, they came up with this concept of original sin – but the woman was just hungry! Makes me laugh really, blaming it all on a woman. The patriarchy,' he scoffs.

God a feminist? This is getting more interesting by the second.

'But I liked the vignettes, the illustrations, the snake, and the modesty and all that,' he says with genuine enthusiasm.

'I see,' I lie. 'So, what about free will? And the doctrine of divine intervention?'

'I've always offered free will. I mean, do people really want some big guy in the sky tying their shoelaces, wiping their noses, telling them what to do? That's a type of servitude, a divine dictatorship. People would be no better than hamsters in a cage. Boredom and terminal ennui would ensue, if not frustration and madness. And besides, I'm a democrat at heart – small "d." Give people boundaries, a civil code if you will, to define acceptable norms of behaviour, then let them go to it.'

'So, the Ten Commandments is a kind of civil code for humanity? And Moses an early day legislator?'

'You could say that,' he says in a non-committal tone.

'So, tell me, how does the doctrine of free will sit with divine intervention?'

'It doesn't.'

'It doesn't?' I'm puzzled, yet again.

'No. I mean, I don't intervene. Divine intervention is all you guys again, not me. You have the freedom to live your lives the way you see fit, make your own choices, make your own mistakes and bear the consequences, whether they be good, bad or indifferent. If I intervene to rectify your mistakes, whether trivial or monumental, then that would run counter to free will. Free will and bearing the consequences that result from exercise of that will, are concomitants.'

'What about the Crucifixion? That would have tested the doctrine of, uh, *non*-divine intervention? After all He was your Son and semi-divine, or wholly divine, or whichever way it was.' I'm not on solid ground when it comes to theological debate, I have to admit. God looks down at the floor, a wistful look crossing his face, and he takes a minute before replying.

'I'm not going to pretend that one wasn't hard. It was really hard, of course it was. He was my Son. Still is my Son, in fact. I'm not afraid to admit, I was on the cusp of doing the "thunderbolt and lightning thing" a thousand times. I wrestled with it all night – my paternal instincts vying with my principles, so to speak. In the end, I couldn't show favouritism or exceptionalism, even for my own Son. I had to show impartiality and that even I'm not above the law, my own law.'

'You say you are, as a matter of principle, and in some senses legally, against acts of favouritism or exceptionalism. But what about the Red Sea and the flight from Egypt?' I ask, still not convinced about this non-divine intervention thing, which runs contrary to everything I've ever read in the Bible – or at least in the Old Testament.

God harrumphs in reply. 'That one! Another one of your constructs. I never parted the Red Sea. The area was geologically unstable, much more so than it is today. There was significant seismic activity on that day that caused a highly unusual water surge, akin to a tsunami. The pursuing Pharaonic forces were actually in boats, not on foot and horse, and consequently, they were deluged, swept away. Bad luck really, well bad luck for the

Pharaoh at any rate.'

So, the Israelites escaped only through interventions of a freak geological event – I draw in a deep breath at that one.

'And you've never intervened in the affairs of man? Never felt compelled to cross your own divine red lines?' I persist.

'Look, let me put it this way,' He says testily. 'Ask Sargent Robert Cryer. Ask Private Ryan O'Toole. Ask 2nd Lieutenant Algernon Farquhar. Ask any of them.'

'Who is, or was, Sargent Robert Cryer?' I ask, perplexed.

'Late of the 7th Battalion, 1st Division, Australian Imperial Force. Died in action, 2nd August, 1916, Western Front.' He pauses and His serenity returns.

'Please continue,' I say encouragingly.

'He died in a fox hole. He was never a believer, certainly not a devout one at any rate. Only ever attended Church for weddings, funerals, those sorts of things – a social church goer you might say and certainly not a man of faith. He wasn't even in Church for his own funeral, poor chap; they never found the body you see. In fact, it lies buried in the Commonwealth war grave at Thiepval – no one knows that, apart from me, of course.'

I detect a hint of melancholy in his voice. He pauses as if for reflection then continues. 'Sergeant Cryer found himself crouching, stranded alone in a fox hole, a particularly shallow fox hole, in a section of No Man's Land after an unsuccessful advance towards the German lines. Fearing a second wave, the Germans laid down blanket fire in that section. Things looked pretty grim for Sergeant Cryer, what with a constant barrage of HE rounds exploding all around him. That's when he did it, what I call the "fox hole moment."' He pauses again.

'The "fox hole moment?"' I repeat.

'Yes. He asked me to save his life, repeatedly, and in return, he promised to become a devout believer, show up at Church every Sunday, give up the booze – even women – and so on. I've heard it a million times, up and down the millennia – everyone's a believer when they think they're about to die.'

'And you didn't intervene?'

'Nope. Not that I wasn't sympathetic, in fact I was sympathetic, don't get me wrong. Bob was actually a good guy, warm, generous, always keeping the men's spirits up. Even shared his rations, meagre as they were. He was from Western Australia. Nice place – apart from the infestations of rabbits and mice – you should consider going there someday. But, ultimately what could I do?'

'You mean self-will and non-intervention?'

'Yup.'

'Hm, okay.' *Well, we've done this topic to death – no pun intended – so not much more needs to be said about it,* I think to myself.

'So, let's turn to a different topic, if we may, maybe one more weighty and down to earth. I'd like to discuss religious differences, different interpretations of faith, and the fundamental part such schisms play in many of the violent conflicts we see on this planet today. Do you feel any sense of responsibility for this?'

I admit I'm not pulling any punches with this question.

'Hmm,' God pauses for thought, unphased. 'All the great monotheistic faiths are actually the same, except in one important point; they differ in their comprehension of me. I leave it up to you to decide how to comprehend me and how you wish to convert that comprehension into religious frameworks and everyday practice. Whether you want to view me as a Muslim, Jewish or Christian God, or if we look at the great Eastern religions such as Buddhism, that's entirely up to you. To me, they're all variations on the same theme. All take their fundamental inspiration from me, in one way or another, which means there's a strong commonality across religions – although, of course, people often choose to ignore this, preferring to accentuate the differences for their own purposes. Take, for instance, the Buddha and Jesus. Both underwent personal fundamental transformative experiences during their "wandering years," eschewing materiality and embracing asceticism. Both formed deep personal tenets during this time that form the bedrock of Christian and Buddhist religious frameworks to this day.'

God leans forward, all animated: 'You see the commonality? So, I don't think it's religious differences per se that drive inter communal conflict, but rather Man's historic and genetic impulses to fend for himself in a hostile world, which means competing with other individuals and groups for the scarce resources on offer. Religion is just an excuse for conflict, not the cause – the underlying reason is competition! You're competitive beasts by nature!'

I raise my eyebrows, noting this is the first time he's referred to us as beasts.

'But we live in a world of plenty today,' I protest, equally animated. 'The supermarket shelves groan with untold sources of protein and other sustenance – so much so that we can all stuff ourselves silly in front of the tele – so how can competition for resources still be a fundamental driver of conflict?'

'Genetic engineering, or rather, faulty genetic engineering,' God replies cooly.

'Genetic engineering?' I raise my eyebrows.

'Yes, genetic engineering was in its infancy during the Creation. In order to enable Man to survive in the pioneer years, in a hostile environment, competition was inevitable given the initial scarcity of resources on the planet. I therefore had to code strong competitive instincts into human DNA. What I didn't do, however, was time bound the lifespan of the competitive gene. In hindsight I should have built in "end of life" into that DNA strand, so that when man had evolved into the supermarket age, the tribalism and warring that are hallmarks of the competitive gene would simply atrophy, just in the same way you don't use your appendix anymore. So, in the age of CostCo and the "all you can eat buffet," we end up with this anomalous situation where man competes against man – often violently – driven by the same historic but redundant desire for food and shelter. But as I said, terra scale genetic engineering was in its infancy back in those days.'

'I see.' I find myself saying this a lot, but in fact, I'm struggling to comprehend. 'So, the great wars and conflicts of history, the untold death and destruction, the senseless slaughter and so on, are all down to nascent and incomplete genetic engineering techniques?'

'Yup. But I've got the hang of it now,' He says with a look of complete innocence and no sense of irony whatsoever.

I scratch my head and plough on.

'You've expressed great tolerance for different religious interpretations of yourself, but so far, you've only framed that tolerance within monotheistic concepts. Do you hold equally tolerant views of polytheism?'

'I'm supportive,' He responds without equivocation. 'Again, it's a matter of interpretation. You say *tom-ar-to* and I say *tom-ay-to,* but we both know we're talking about the red berry of the plant Solanum Lycopersicum. Interpretation of the divine and its religious expression is driven by a host of factors, including differences in stages of human development, climate and geography, relationship with natural resources, language, underlying socio-political precepts, economics, and so on. In fact, animism for example, is a very practical interpretation of the divine, given the importance of plant-based food sources to the well-being of agrarian societies.'

God is displaying David Attenborough-like relish for this topic, I note. 'Before the advent and widespread adoption of monotheism, I was a fan of polytheism. I mean some of it was just downright creative, a credit to the fertile and adaptive imagination of man.'

He pauses for a moment. 'If you look at the Hellenic Pantheon, it was rich and colourful and beautifully designed for the needs of the time, and people were much more religiously observant than today's adherents of monotheism. Why? Because religion was the means of making the inexplicable explicable. Before the widespread embrace of empirical observation and science, how did you explain lightning, for example? Well, you couldn't, not in the sense you can today, so, hey presto, you created Zeus. By the way, I was a big fan of Zeus, quite admired his looks and the way the Renaissance masters used him as an inspiration for my likeness on church ceilings and such.'

I'm tempted to ask him who his favourite Renaissance master is but decide against it.

'Having said that, some of this went too far, I mean a God of Tricks, Dolos, that's really stretching the bow. And Janus, the two-faced God? And what about that guy who slaughtered bulls, Mithras – none of that's really me you know.'

He sounds peeved, so I quickly change the subject, hurtling forward from the ancient to the modern.

'If you look at today's political, social and economic outlook, we face unprecedented challenges on many fronts, including the breakdown of the postwar world order. We've seen the retreat of democracy and the return of strong man politics, nativism, tribalism, geopolitical rivalries, a global economy addicted to cheap debt and of course the climate crisis and the recent pandemic. If you add this all up, it begs the obvious question: Are we close to the Revelation, to the Apocalypse, to the Second Coming?'

'Hmm,' God muses, tapping His chin in a thoughtful way. 'Well, fundamentally I'm an optimist. I think modern day pundits are overly given to pessimism. The outlook remains overwhelmingly positive in my opinion, particularly if you look at historical benchmarks. For instance, you mention strong man politics. Yes, I get that, but if you view today's political landscape through an historical lens, the situation is actually quite bright. Why do I say this? Look back only as far as the nineteen forties, and you had the unholy quad of Hitler, Stalin, Mussolini and Franco; some of the most egregious despots and mass murderers known to man. Then, add on thirty years or so, and you can add in Pol Pot, Pinochet and others to the Pantheon of Evil. So, do you really think we're on the eve of destruction?'

I notice God is becoming really animated at this point in our conversation, but then suddenly, dropping into a deadpan tone and lowering his voice, he states conspiratorially: 'I knew

Gavrilo Princip.'

'You knew Gavrilo Princip?' I echo, taken aback. Where did that one come from? 'You mean the guy who assassinated the Austrian archduke in Sarajevo, triggering World War One, that Gavrilo Princip?'

'Yes, that guy.'

'I see.' I reply lamely.

'Do you?' God challenges, clearly reading the lost look on my face.

'Well, OK, maybe let's hear it from you just to make sure we're all clear.'

'Well, there was a flourishing cross-dressing scene going on in Sarajevo at that time – combined with homo eroticism – all dressed up as the Avant Garde. The city was a shining light of liberal experimentation in the Austro-Hungarian empire – much more so than Vienna or Budapest. Princip was a luminary in that scene.'

'Okay. I must admit, I'm a little lost now,' I say.

'His nom-de-couture was "Eve."'

He looks at me expectantly, but I imagine all He sees is a dumb look staring back at him.

'Don't you see? We've been on the *Eve* of destruction many times before, but Man always bounces back!' God states triumphantly with a hint of mischief in his eyes.

I mumble something unintelligible in response. Is this some sort of puerile humour, or are divine conversational twists just beyond my mortal sense of conversational convention? I make a show of straightening my notes then clear my throat, eager to return to firmer ground.

'But what about climate change? Man hasn't always had the wherewithal to poison the planet in the way that he has today – that's a new phenomenon, surely?'

'Maybe so, but what the Earth is experiencing today is trivial compared to previous climate crises. Again, this is just another manifestation of Man's propensity to always believe he lives in the worst possible time in history. It's a form of conceit and inflated self-importance really,' He says somewhat disparagingly.

'Can you expand on that?'

'There are two climate crises that make everything else that has since been, or will be, simply irrelevant. The first is the Ice Age, or to be more accurate, the Ice Ages, when continental-size glaciers covered enormous regions of the Earth, associated with Milankovitch cycles. The second is the Cretaceous-Paleogene event, a mass extinction in which seventy-five percent of plant and animal species on Earth were wiped out, caused by the Chicxulub impactor striking Earth. Now, that's not to say the current climate crisis is of no concern, it certainly is, and it doesn't bode well for the next several generations, but when you've been around as long as I have – and I'll continue to be around for a long time yet – everything is relative.' He smiles serenely.

I want to ask Him about his own carbon footprint but hold back in case it comes across as disrespectful.

'Well, we're unfortunately coming to the end of what I must say has been a, err, most fascinating conversation.' I clear my throat. 'So, that leaves us with the final and possibly largest topic to discuss.'

'Oh that,' He shrugs with obvious disdain, looking away from me.

I carry on unperturbed. 'The one question that is on everyone's mind, not just now but since the dawn of time.' Drum roll in my head, here goes: 'What is the meaning of...life... the universe...and everything? In other words: WHY ARE WE HERE? What's the point of it all?' There, it's out in the open.

'You should ask Arthur Dent.' A hint of a smile creases the corners of His mouth – a personal joke perhaps?

'Arthur Dent?' I respond puzzled. Is he referring to the main character in the novel "The Hitchhiker's Guide to the Galaxy?"

'No, no, it's nothing,' He says, brushing it aside quickly. 'It never ceases to amaze me how your lot is always searching for meaning: meaning in the bottom of a teacup; meaning in the entrails of a bird; meaning in a crystal ball; meaning in a ballpoint pen. It never ends,' He scoffs. 'What is it with *meaning*? Are you all so restless and hollow that you can only feel complete if you find meaning beyond yourselves? Let me offer you a parable then – I'm good at those you know,' He says with a wry smile.

'There was a powerful potentate that ruled a land in what we call today the Middle East...and I won't tell you which land, to avoid inflaming any tensions.' He smiles mischievously. 'He had everything his potent heart could desire: riches beyond imagination; strength; health; and good looks; the love and respect – or maybe fear – of his people; suzerainty over lands from desert to ocean; marvels of engineering and architecture; and so on. But after a while, it wasn't enough. Yet another glorious foreign conquest, or one more palace of untold opulence, failed to fill the inner hollowness that was gnawing away at him, like some wasting disease.

'He consulted the royal astrologers, the priests, the shamans, the charlatans, the oracles, and even in desperation a mountain lion! But despite it all, no one could offer him what he craved most: self-fulfilment through finding...you guessed it... the meaning of his life. Finally, in desperation he turned to a wizened old man, a ragged old thing, bent over and wearied, hobbling on a stick, smelling worse than a goat – you know the type – who arrived at the royal palace one day claiming he had untold treasure to offer the potentate. The old man was finally granted an audience and told the potentate that he would show him how to find the meaning of his life.

'"How so?" Asked the Potentate. To which the old man replied, the only thing you must do is close your eyes and open them only when I tell you to do so. The potentate, while doubtful, nonetheless agreed. The old man shuffled off in the direction of the royal bedroom, leading the potentate by his hand. Once inside the room, the old man locked the door behind him, guided the potentate into position and bid him open his eyes. The potentate was at first bewildered at the image that greeted him, and his bewilderment soon turned to rage.

'"What is the meaning of this, you old fool!" raged the Potentate. "You asked me to show you the meaning of your life and I have done just that," replied the old man calmly. "But it's a mirror!" fumed the Potentate. Yes, and in the mirror is the meaning of your life, answered the old man. In a fit of rage, the Potentate unsheathed his scimitar and chopped off the old man's head there and then.'

God pauses. 'Now, many years later, in fact on his deathbed, the potentate recalled the old man and his trickery, and then the penny suddenly dropped! What he saw in the mirror all those years ago, was in fact the meaning of his life, the old man was right: he *himself* was the meaning of his life – his whole purpose in life was to discover himself.' God folds his arms, a look of complete serenity descending upon him.

I pause to take this in, turn it around in my mind and after a while ruminating on it, I speak: 'So, do you mean to say that the purpose of life is staring back at us in the mirror every morning when we brush our teeth, that we – ourselves – are the meaning of life?'

Can it really be so prosaic? I think to myself feeling somewhat deflated and disappointed. Surely there must be a deeper mystery to life waiting to be unlocked? A mirror, come on!

'Yes. Stop looking for that which cannot be found beyond yourself. The search for existential meaning is only the sign of a restless soul – trust me, I've known a few souls,' He says as an aside. 'There is no universal or mystical puzzle waiting to be solved. There is no holy grail of meaning out there in the wide yonder – that is simply the fools' gold of personal quests. Better to keep your VW camper van parked in the garage and instead go into a dark room to contemplate the self. Once you've found that meaning, you've found inner peace, and once you've found inner peace, you've found the divine. The riches of a peaceful soul – being at peace with oneself – are beyond any earthly wealth. The wealthy man can only ever be poor; a Sisyphean soul doomed forever to labour uphill in the search of more.'

He leans towards me, beckoning me closer and enigmatically whispers in my ear: 'Without you, there is no Me and without Me, there is no you. That is the meaning of...life...the universe...and everything.'

A CONVERSATION WITH GAIUS JULIUS CAESAR

'So why did you do it?' I ask.

'To save the Republic. There was no higher duty than to save the Republic,' he proclaims with total self-belief.

'I find that ironic, given you essentially emasculated the Republic and laid the foundations for imperial rule for the next five hundred years. But let's come back to that later,' I retort.

Caesar offers me a condescending smile in return and continues unfazed. 'Crossing the Rubicon was essentially an act of national rejuvenation, to Make Rome Great Again, if you will. Pompey and the Senate were stealing elections and ruling the Republic for personal political gain – they cared nothing for the people or the dignity of Rome. The whole system was rotten. Rome was dying of its corruption, and the Senate was its decaying heart, feebly beating, only rising from its sick bed when it must, to obstruct any innovation that would challenge its self-interest.'

He pauses and leans back in his curule chair. 'So, while I thought long and hard about the consequences of the Senate's decree ordering me to stay north of the Rubicon, I felt I had little choice but to cross the river with the Thirteenth Legion. And to be clear, to me it wasn't an act imbued with the fatalistic "point of no return" you give the phrase today; my intention was always to parlay with the Senate and was never a declaration of war. In fact, at the time I took a massive gamble. I believed that if the Senate didn't engage in negotiations with me, I risked defeat on the battlefield.'

I raise my eyebrows in surprise.

'Yes, the Thirteenth was the most battle-hardened legion

in the Roman army and had just defeated the Gauls at Alesia,' he says with obvious pride. 'But it was still only one legion against at least four that Pompey had raised, and I'd fought with some of his men in the war against Spartacus, so I knew they could wield a sword. In fact, if it had come to battle, I'd even considered re-crossing the Rubicon to join up with the legions I'd left behind in the north. I was therefore surprised, very surprised, when Pompey abandoned Rome so soon after I crossed. It was a colossal strategic mistake in my opinion. My position was much weaker than he knew.

'Why? Once I crossed into Roman Italy, I feared many of my veterans would simply desert, being so close to home and the promise of retirement after ten years of hard campaigning. So, as I said, crossing the Rubicon was a major gamble, but a gamble that ultimately played out to my benefit. Fortune favours her own,' he adds, a gleam of pride and defiance in his eyes.

'Make Rome Great Again? Save the people from the Senate? That all sounds like unashamed political propaganda to me, dressing up your own ambitions as a noble patriotic cause,' I challenge him. 'Your whole history points to naked political ambition and your singular pursuit of power. Was not the conquest of Gaul simply a campaign to increase your popularity back in Rome and help get you elected to the highest office in the land? After all, there's nothing like a daring military campaign to propel a Roman political career – you more than most knew that only too well,' I state testily, deliberately challenging Caesar's legendary composure.

'Well,' he pauses, smoothing a fold in his toga, without the slightest sign of annoyance, 'you can't separate personal political ambition from pursuit of a higher purpose. Without achieving high office, without the executive power it confers, you don't have the means at your disposal to achieve your purpose.'

Hmm, sounds like a spin on the age-old argument that the means justify the end, I think to myself. Nevertheless, I decide to leave it unchallenged.

'So, shifting gears slightly, how do you compare today's

politicians to those of your time, say, the likes of Cicero, Cato, and even yourself?'

Caesar nods approvingly, suggesting he likes the question.

'Today, you have some very strong politicians displaying great purpose and vision, able to galvanize their societies and push forward with their agendas. Take Recep Tayyip Erdoğan, Vladimir Putin, Donald Trump, for instance. All incredibly strong leaders – although Trump is in a slightly different league, of course,' he adds, with a knowing smile. 'If you look at Erdoğan, he has a very clear vision for Turkey's place in the Middle East and Eastern Mediterranean – the "Century of Turkey" no less. He's successfully positioning his country as a dominant regional player, a power broker with a seat at the top table, extending his influence and control abroad, creating a new imperium no less.

'I particularly admire how he's established a presidential role for himself, increasing the powers of the executive, so he can get things done. It's very similar to my proclamation as "dictator perpetuo," or Dictator for Life, in 44 BC,' he states approvingly. 'And he's also got his legislative assembly under control, like I did with the Roman Senate, so he can pursue policies for the good of the people without interference from vested factional interests. His ruthless pursuit of corrupt politicians also echoes my own prosecution of provincial governors, notorious for their extortion and corruption. In fact, it would be no surprise if he's studied my career, and in some ways, modelled his success on mine,' he adds with no hint of modesty.

'You then have Putin, who is purposefully reasserting Russia's status as a great power, through a mixture of realpolitik and military force. His power projection into the Middle East, for example, was both clinical and strategic, injecting himself into a central position in places like Syria and making Russia relevant again. Reminds me of my own campaigns in Asia Minor – although I understand things have slightly unravelled recently for him,' he adds with a hint of regret, no doubt referring to the rapidly shifting geopolitics in the Middle East that have not favoured Russia.

'Now Trump, while of similar instincts to Erdoğan and Putin, is not as, err, *conventional*. But he is, however, hamstrung by his legislature – or at least was in his first term – in the same way I was before I became Dictator for Life. My advice to him would be to hollow out both the House and the Senate as independent chambers and pack them with people dependent on his grace and favours. Then he's got a chance of executing his agenda – that's the only way to get things done!'

'So, it's fair to say you're not a proponent of a democratic system of government,' I state testily, boggled by his cynicism.

'People need to be led,' Caesar continues, without breaking his stride. 'They need to be led by strong leaders. They don't need the exercise of democratic freedoms. Look where that's leading today: you see gridlocked and enfeebled government everywhere you turn, a complete inability to undertake necessary but uncomfortable change. And what do you get instead? Populism, nativism, racial tensions, short-term thinking for electoral gain. People don't need to elect their leaders at the ballot box. People need bread and circuses! There's nothing like a good day out in the arena to keep people happy,' he smiles benevolently.

'Would you throw Christians to the lions too?' I interject, sarcastically.

'I think we're beyond that, don't you?' he replies, narrowing his eyes and smiling at me. 'Strong leadership that seeks to serve the people, improving their daily lives, keeping the cost of bread down, that's the most appropriate form of government. Look at the land redistribution programs I initiated for example,' he says enthusiastically, leaning towards me. 'Cohorts of the poor were raised out of poverty and enabled to feed themselves and their families. And this policy rested on forced appropriation of land, and it could never have happened with an independently minded legislature standing in the way. The entrenched forces of privilege would have blocked it in the Senate – Cato would have probably worked up one of his filibusters.' Caesar groans, having been on the receiving end of many a Cato "late night special."

Okay, so I think it's fairly clear where Caesar sits on the political spectrum, but there is so much more to the man than politics. He's the second greatest general in history – according to Napoleon, who accords himself first place – a mighty orator who enthralled the Forum, a brilliant prosecutor and a moderately successful author. And then of course, his prowess between the sheets. *So, let's go hunting,* I think with a smile.

'Okay, so let's move to topics less politically charged, shall we?' I pause for a moment because I'm about to take another stab at the mighty Caesar's legendary composure. 'To this day, when we think of the great love affairs of ancient history, we always think of Mark Antony and Cleopatra,' I smile insinuatingly. 'Yet you too had a colourful relationship with the Queen of the Nile, but somehow, "Caesar and Cleopatra" just doesn't roll off the tongue, does it? So, was Mark Antony simply a better lover than you?'

Caesar regards me cooly for a moment, fixing me with his intense black eyes and then chuckles.

'Cle-o-pat-ra,' he rolls her name around his tongue, almost like an American movie star from the 1930's. 'Well, that was one amazing woman,' he exclaims, admiringly. 'You could hear a pin drop when she walked into a room. She was entrancing. People simply fell under her spell. They were completely captivated by her, enslaved even. I've never met any woman remotely like her and probably never will. Well, except maybe for one, Margaret Thatcher,' he corrects himself, with a sheepish grin. 'But,' he continues in a haughty tone, 'I was completely immune to her charm.'

'Margaret Thatcher or Cleopatra?' I ask, slightly confused

'Cleopatra of course! Who could be immune to Margaret's charm?'

Obviously, he's a fan of the Iron Lady I note.

'Yes, I could see straight through Cleopatra. She was a mistress of theatrics. She had an exceptional talent for playing to her audience. She knew exactly how to flatter them, how to pander to their egos, tease out their hidden desires. She was the greatest show woman on earth, and it was all about bending people to her will.' He pauses and smiles fondly. 'I first met her rolled up in a carpet, you know,' he exclaims somewhat randomly.

'In a carpet? Was she selling Persian rugs?' I reply, with a touch of sarcasm.

'Well, yes, and no. It was more like she was selling herself.'

I raise my eyebrows.

'Let me explain,' he says with a broad smile. 'Late one evening, several Egyptians entered my quarters carrying a carpet. They unrolled it on the floor and out popped Cleopatra. I was both amazed and amused, momentarily at a loss for words. Of course, her reputation preceded her, so I had a good idea of who she was. But first impressions count. What an entrance! However, it didn't take long for me to see through her act, despite the flattery and subtle seduction. I knew she needed my help to have any chance of claiming the throne from her brother,' he explains, before pausing for a moment.

'She actually seduced me,' he continues, with a hint of pride. 'She practically threw herself at me, after plying me with wine and sweet conversation. She pushed me onto the bed, sat on top of me, and as they say, the rest is history,' he exclaims beaming.

Lucky Julius, I think to myself.

'And to be brutally honest,' he continues, 'she wasn't beautiful, not in the conventional sense. She had a prominent hooked nose that you could almost hang a cloak on. Not really my type; I prefer the aquiline Roman nose,' he says, tapping his own. 'Now, I'm not saying I didn't have feelings for her – because I did. But I was clear-eyed about our relationship; it was a blend of passion and politics. Moreover, I was inclined to support her cause in the sibling rivalry tearing Egypt apart at the time.' He pauses, frowning, his mood suddenly darkening. 'Her brother, a few days earlier, had presented me with Pompey's head on a platter – quite literally – hoping to ingratiate himself with me. I was horrified,' he says, a mixture of disgust and anger in his voice.

'But Pompey was your sworn enemy,' I protest. 'He'd just spent the last four years trying to kill you in the civil war, so wasn't this a boon to you?' Caesar fixes me with a look of cool contempt.

'Pompey was a noble Roman, a former brother in arms and my son-in-law. It was an act of gross barbarity, an affront to dignity and rank. I've seen many horrors on the battlefield, but this was beyond the pale. In fact, when I saw his severed head, I wept.' Caesar blinks and rubs his eyes. 'It was there and then that I decided Ptolemy's fate, not that he knew it at the time.'

He sighs and pauses for a few moments, before suddenly and unexpectedly springing back to the topic: 'So, was Mark Antony a better lover? He was certainly a more famous lover. Let's be realistic, if your wife kills herself by thrusting a cobra to her breast, then you're bound to get better press, no competition! And besides, I blame Shakespeare,' Caesar states emphatically, folding his arms.

'You blame Shakespeare?' I ask, surprised that the Bard has suddenly entered the conversation.

'Yes. The Bard never let historical accuracy get in the way of a good story. An asp!' he scoffs. 'Have you ever tried to handle an Egyptian cobra? Let me tell you, you'd never get one close to your chest. Its strike range is five feet; as soon as you tried to take a hold of it, you'd be bitten on your hands and arms, and within seconds, you'd start to experience neuromuscular discoordination, dizziness, and ocular deterioration. Cleopatra was the most determined and strongest woman I've ever known – apart from Margaret, maybe,' he adds, softening. 'But even she couldn't pull that one off!'

'Sounds like you know a thing or two about serpents. So, how *did* she die then?'

'She took poison. She mixed it with wine. It was a quick acting neurotoxin that killed her in seconds – she always made sure she had a vial on her. Cleopatra was unemotional about death, even expected to die young given her Ptolemaic lineage and the violent times she lived in. You know, she also identified as the earthly embodiment of the Goddess Isis – mainly for political reasons – but she crossed the line at some point and started to actually believe she was the Goddess and would ascend to Heaven upon her death. As I said, she was an unusual woman.'

He shakes his head a little sadly and pauses before brightening up again. 'Having said that, Mark Antony and I were closer than either of us ever was to her,' he states, surprising me.

On impulse, given the whiff of scandal that has always dogged his love life, I shoot out an audacious question, wincing in anticipation of a negative reaction: 'So were you and Mark Antony lovers then?'

Caesar contemplates me for a moment, narrowing his eyes and tensing his face, before suddenly laughing in a dismissive manner. 'Where on earth did you get such a preposterous idea from?'

I avoid eye contact with him and flick through my notes. 'If we go back to your early military career in Asia minor, in 80 BC you were sent to the kingdom of Bithynia, situated on the Northwest coast of modern-day Turkey, to requisition ships for Rome's campaign against the city state of Miletus. And you secured those ships from Bithynia's ruler, King Nicomedes, in less than a week, yet' – I pause for effect – 'you lingered at court for a whole month before returning to your legion. Your commander, Marcus Thermus, was livid, publicly dressing you down and practically accusing you of desertion. So, it leads me to assume you must have had a very good reason to dally for so long and risk a court martial,' I state insinuatingly.

'And your point is?' he replies with insouciance, examining his nails.

'Nicomedes' court was renowned for its eastern exoticism, its decadence, and dare I say, its debauchery. It's well known that he surrounded himself with athletic young Greek and Roman boys and liked to dress up as Alexander the Great at his bacchanalias. He barely hid his numerous homosexual affairs, and his lust for his male household slaves was legendary.

It was into this febrile environment you landed; an impressionable young officer eager to complete his first major mission, by any means necessary. And on the other side of this transaction, you had the lecherous old King, all too eager to deflower a noble young Roman, especially one with such an illustrious lineage. Add all this up and you get your infamous tryst with Nicomedes. A tryst that not only dogged your career but became the first of many male love affairs throughout your life, including that with Mark Antony, another serial philanderer!'

I pause to gauge his reaction. Caesar looks me straight in the eye, cool and calm, unmoved by my accusations, except for a faint flinch of his jaw. He takes his time to consider his reply, running his fingers through his hair.

'You're simply recycling hackneyed old gossip that was scotched millennia ago; slander peddled by my political enemies to discredit me – a not uncommon tactic in Roman politics, I may add. But what you fail to mention, as did my enemies, is that the time I spent in Bithynia was entirely consistent with my mission. The political situation was complex,' he states, leaning towards me, his tone serious. 'The ruler of the neighbouring Black Sea kingdom of Pontus – located in the North of modern-day Turkey – had lifelong designs on Bithynia, despite its status as a Roman protectorate. Therefore, my mission didn't go unnoticed, you might say.'

'And what does geopolitics have to do with your dalliance at court?' I cut in, not wanting to be led off topic.

'As you said,' he continues, 'Nicomedes had agreed to give me my ships. I was preparing to set sail for Miletus with the fleet, when without warning the old man reneged on our deal. Just like that. Totally out of the blue.' He frowns. 'And there was *no* way I was returning to Thermus without those ships,' he states emphatically, sitting upright.

'So, what was going on?' I ask with a hint of cynicism, thinking of what the young Caesar and the old lecher were really up to.

'A certain piece of intelligence came to hand,' he smiles

softly. 'Mine was not the only mission in the palace as it turned out. The ruler of Pontus, King Mithridates, had sent his son Pharnaces to Bithynia just after me in total secrecy. Once I learnt of this, through my own agents in court, I flushed him out and sent him and his men packing in sackcloth back to Pontus, along with a message for his father. Nicomedes was weak and swung in the wind. With Pharnaces gone and no longer threatening him – forcing him to withhold the ships – it was a simple matter to get him to honour our original agreement.'

'Hmm, I see. And why is this only coming to light now?' I ask, arching my eyebrows, not recalling any mention of this in my research.

'Because I've just declassified it,' he states with supreme confidence.

'I'll have to take your word for it then, won't I. But I'm curious. You also said you sent a message to King Mithridates, via his son. What was that?'

'Oh, something along the lines that it would be wise not to cross me or Rome again,' he states matter-of-factly, picking at some lint on his scarlet cloak.

'An idle threat?' I wonder aloud.

'No, not really. I paid a visit to Pontus in 48 BC and annihilated the Pontian army,' he states casually, the lint now gone.

'Your bore a grudge for thirty-two years?' I ask, somewhat astonished.

'I don't bear grudges. I don't believe in them,' he replies coolly. 'I was honouring my word. Pontus did cross me again, and Roman rule relied upon our subjects and enemies knowing there would be consequences, without fail, for bad faith. I more than anyone upheld that principle as inviolate,' he states with a haughty tone.

'You may know,' he adds as an aside, 'I was captured by pirates in my youth, when I was crossing the sea from Brindisi to Rhodes. The fools had the temerity to try and ransom me for twenty talents of silver – *twenty*, for *me*, Caesar! Can you imagine such an insult!' he states, with a mixture of disgust and astonishment, while tossing his head back, nose up in the air – which I can attest is a fine Roman proboscis. 'But rest assured, I soon set them straight, upping it to *fifty*, far closer to my true worth,' he sniffs. 'But I also offered them something far more valuable than silver. Something priceless in fact. But what did they do? They scoffed at me, falling about the deck laughing – the imbeciles!'

'And what did you offer them that was so priceless?' I ask my curiosity piqued.

'Their lives! I told them if they released me immediately, I would be clement and spare them, but if they continued to hold me hostage, I would crucify every single one of them and sell their families into slavery. But of course, the dolts chose the money – obviously they didn't know who they were dealing with. And as soon as I was released, once the ransom was paid, I immediately raised a task force and sailed back to Pharmacusa, the island they held where they held me, off the western coast of Turkey. The pirates were either arrogant, or stupid, or both, because they were still there at anchor when I arrived. I did, however, show them some mercy despite the fact they spurned my offer.'

'You did? Why was that?'

'Because after all was said and done, they weren't *complete* barbarians – they had actually managed to appreciate my oratory, which I practised in front of them during my time in captivity, much to my surprise.'

'Really?' I say, also surprised, at his mercy, not his oratory.

'Yes. I slit their throats before crucifying them; a much quicker and kinder way to die,' he states, with no hint of irony. 'You see, respect for Roman rule had to be upheld and very visibly so.'

We've digressed into pirates and enforcing the "Pax Romana," which as interesting as it is, is a diversion from the main topic of Caesar's affairs with Mark Antony, Nicomedes, and many others. I glance at my notes, before bringing us back onto topic.

'Even your own men, your beloved Thirteenth, at your

Gallic Triumph in Rome, sang that now infamous bawdy verse: "Gallias Caesar subegit, Caesarem Nicomedes," meaning of course: "Caesar laid the Gauls low but Nicomedes laid Caesar lower." And furthermore, you never shook off your unofficial royal title as "The Queen of Bithynia," did you?'

Caesar chuckles, a warm expression on his face. 'Soldiers will be soldiers,' he says fondly. Then, with a flick of his head, he adds mockingly: 'Politicians will be politicians. Scurrilous bunch really.'

'Your love affair with Mamurra, your Praefectus Fabrum during the Gallic wars and expedition to Britain is well documented by your contemporary Catullus,' I continue undeterred.

'Catullus,' Caesar harrumphs. 'The most scurrilous poet to ever disgrace Rome and a sexual degenerate to boot,' he states with a hint of bitterness. 'In fact, if you're interested to know, Catullus' own personal life was a tale of iniquity, and as for his poetry, it was the best expression of moral debasement ever written in the Latin language – an epitome of the man himself! But to be honest,' he continues, softening his tone, 'I found him rather amusing in a pathetic sort of way. I even invited him to dinner after he apologized and withdrew that bilious nonsense about me,' he says, with a look of condescension on his face.

There's no ruffling Caesar's feathers, I must admit. He remains unperturbed, effortlessly deflecting every barb I throw his way. If truth be told, I'm starting to feel a bit foolish, even pedantic, in my relentless pursuit of this topic. So, with a glance at the clock, I decide it's time to shift gears to a subject that might finally unsettle Caesar. I take a sip of water and clear my throat.

'So, let's move on from your personal life and discuss that most infamous and public of events, if we may?'

Caesar narrows his eyes, a hint of discomfort flickering across his face.

'You'd been declared Dictator in Perpetuo – Dictator for Life – by the Senate, reaching the pinnacle of your political career. You were about to embark on your most ambitious military campaign yet, against the Parthian Empire, in what is now modern-day Iran. Additionally, you were on the verge of compelling the Senate to enact a slew of political, economic, and social reforms. Rome and the known world were at your feet, yours to mould and potentially change history as we know it today.' I pause for effect, leaning toward him. 'And then, the cliff edge looms suddenly: the bad dreams, the entrails and omens, the Ides of March, Pompey's Theatre –

all of which culminate in the most infamous assassination in history, arguably an assassination more shocking and resonant to this day than the slayings of Thomas à Becket, Lincoln, Gandhi, and Kennedy. But what remains an enduring mystery is why you ignored all the warning signs, both divine and mortal, of which there were plenty, and instead walked almost willingly into the trap, like a lamb to the slaughter.'

I note Caesar is shifting uncomfortably in his curule chair now.

'Even in February of that year, the omens didn't look good leading up to the Ides of March. At the Lupercalia, you sacrificed a bull whose heart had a hyper single ventricle defect. The next day, your priest oversaw another sacrifice hoping for better omens, but the animal had an inflamed hepatic liver, and he warned you that these signs could only mean one thing: death, your death, one month later on the Ides of March. Yet, you blithely ignored him. Even on the very morning of your assassination – a month later to the day, as forewarned – you attended another sacrifice overseen by the same priest, when yet again the animal's organs were diseased and so rotten that the signs of doom were unequivocal. But what did you do? You teased the priest, telling him that his prophecies must be wrong since today was the Ides of March and yet no harm had come to you! But, he warned you that the month was not over until the bell rang at midnight!' I exclaim, maddened at the almost suicidal disregard Caesar displayed for all of these warnings.

'Priests and seers! Half-witted old men babbling nonsense. Do you really think the future can be told by examining the entrails of an animal? It's just a cheap card trick. On balance of probabilities, they're bound to get it right now and again,' Caesar scoffs, cutting in.

'But could you so easily dismiss the warnings from Calpurnia, your wife? Or even those in your own head? When the Ides dawned on that fateful March day, Calpurnia awoke in terror, having dreamt she'd held your bloodied body in her arms. Fearing for your life, she begged you not to leave home that morning. Your dreams too had also been alarming – you dreamt of flying through the air and shaking hands with Jupiter! But yet, you still pushed all concerns aside,' I state with a mix of passion and frustration.

'Irrational women and muddled dreams – what use do I have for them!' he scoffs again.

'Okay, then if we agree for a moment that divine portents are reasonably dismissed as superstitious nonsense, then what about more earthly warnings? You had an extensive intelligence gathering network that spanned the Roman empire and in Rome itself you could rely on a dense network of allies, informers and spies. It was even said you knew about events across the empire almost as they happened, sometimes even before the local governors were aware. The assassination plot was not hatched overnight. It brewed for a number of months with several dozen conspirators in its inner and outer circles across the city.

'Overheard conversations, rumours and second-hand information would undoubtedly have been reported to you. It would have been almost impossible for the conspirators to conceal their deliberations, however carefully they tried. Several informers, in fact, brought you bits of information, that when pieced together, confidently pointed to a possible senatorial plot against your life. Even Brutus, given he was ambivalent about the plot and held suspicions that he was your illegitimate son, tried to warn you in a roundabout way when you dined with him a few weeks earlier.

'And finally, on the very hour of your assassination, Artemidorus of Knidos thrust a scroll at you, detailing the plot against your life but you chose to ignore it!' I exclaim, with increasing frustration. 'I can therefore only conclude that you had a reasonable idea of the plot against you, if not the details of time and place. Your reckless disregard for your life can only point to one of two possible reasons that led you to Pompey's Theatre, the place of your assassination, that morning: your legendary arrogance convinced you that no harm could possibly ever come to you, or there was another reason.' I pause, regarding him, waiting for his reaction.

'Which is?' He responds with feigned disinterest, inspecting the folds in his toga.

'Which is, you were dying!'

Caesar raises his eyebrows, which I notice for the first time are finely plucked.

'Your health was deteriorating so rapidly, that death was inevitable, whether it came from a fatal seizure, or the end of a dagger. And of course, what better ending than an infamous murder that would immortalize you in history; crown your status as the people's hero; achieve your apotheosis; and seal the fate of the Republic and your senatorial enemies once and for all. Many of your friends even stated that your health was rapidly declining in early 44 BC, and you yourself were heard to say on several occasions that you did not wish to live much longer. In fact, only days before your assassination, when dining with Marcus Lepidus, the conversation turned to the ideal death and you stated: "let it come swiftly and unexpectedly" and "better to die gloriously than fade ignominiously into history on a sick bed."'

'That's stretching a longbow. You're an imaginative fellow aren't you,' he replies chuckling. But I suspect a hint of false bravado in his tone.

'Your congenital health problems, your "morbus comitialis," were well known to your contemporaries and later chroniclers, all of whom make reference to a sickness that plagued you in your later years. Suetonius tells of "sudden fainting fits and nightmares." Appian describes "convulsions." And Plutarch tells of you suffering from "distemper in the head" and "epileptic fits." According to him, you collapsed while on campaign in Cordoba in 46 and you later had to retire from the field at Thapsus when "his usual sickness laid hold of him." In the months leading up to your assassination, Calpurnia reported frequent bouts of "weakness in his limbs, dizziness and headaches." And then, of course, there was the infamous public scandal – noted by Cicero – during the Senatorial bestowing of honours in February 44 BC, and I quote: "the Senate and people were scandalized by his haughty insistence to remain seated, as the honours were presented." But of course, they were unaware of the fact that your failure to stand was due to you being "speedily shaken and whirled about, bringing on giddiness and insensibility."'

'They were nothing, merely heavy colds,' Caesar snorts dismissively, but maybe unconvincingly.

'I contend,' pausing for an imaginary drum roll, 'that you suffered from cerebrovascular disease. All of the symptoms reported in your later life are compatible with someone suffering from multiple minor strokes, most likely Transient Ischemic Attacks. Furthermore, you inherited a genetic disposition to the disease; both your father and paternal uncle having died from cardiac arrest. And let me quote Pliny, writing of your father's untimely death: "he bent down to place his shoes upon his feet, clutching suddenly at his breast and falling down dead." I'm certain that if we conducted an MRI of your carotid artery, we'd see clear signs of atherosclerosis.' I pause and Caesar sighs, a dark look crossing his face as he slumps into his curule chair, as if borne down by a heavy weight.

'You've got it wrong. All wrong. It was never about my health,' he states, resignedly.

'How so, wrong?' I challenge him.

'I was betrayed,' he replies in a flat voice.

'You were betrayed? Yes of course you were betrayed! We all know that,' I retort impatiently.

'No, you don't understand. I was betrayed, but by those who were closest to me.'

'You mean Brutus and Cassius?' I state with some irritation.

'No. Well yes, them of course, but there was something else, something that's never been spoken of.' He stops, hesitant.

'Go on,' I say encouragingly, noticing the deflated look about Caesar.

'There are no existing records, and none of the usual chroniclers make any reference to it. Only one person, other than me, was fully aware of the truth surrounding the events of that day, and when he committed suicide that truth died with him, a truth so disturbing that it remains buried in the bowels of history to this day.' He pauses, letting out a long sigh before continuing. 'The Senate had to be abolished. The senatorial class was an implacable enemy of change. Their parochial self-interest was woven into the fabric of Roman society and politics. They owned the land; they supplied the magistrates and governors; they could raise legions at will; they were dominant in trade, shipping and agriculture; in other words, they *were* Rome. I had a program of change spanning the political, social and economic – change that was deeply anathema to the senatorial class's interests.

'Put simply, despite their growing impotence, they had the practical means to stymie, if not kill, any real change. Take, for example, my plans for expanding land distribution. Members of the Senate owned over ninety percent of all farming land, land that I needed to compulsorily acquire for my veterans and the urban poor, to create a system of small holdings that would bind them to the state, by giving them a stake in the state – not unlike Margaret's sale of council housing to their tenants,' he adds as an aside. 'In late 45 BC I therefore began to think about how to abolish the Senate. I was careful, however, to share my thoughts with no one other than two of my closest confidantes, for obvious reasons.'

'And those confidantes where?' I ask.

'Mark Antony and Gaius Octavius, my great nephew. Together we debated different options, including an armed insurrection, physically invading the chamber – after all there was a precedent – followed by summary imprisonment, expulsion, and even execution of certain recalcitrant senators. We had the numbers in terms of loyal legions, both in Rome and the provinces. However, we eliminated this option, as we'd just come through the upheaval of the civil war, and we didn't want any more bloodshed, given the Senate could still rely on a few legions of its own. We also considered issuing an extraordinary dictatorial decree to temporarily suspend the Senate, with a view to turning the suspension into a permanent dissolution over time. But the people were still wary of anyone wielding absolute power in Rome, and we feared this might create sympathy for the Senate and breed popular resistance.'

'But *you* were extremely popular with the people, were you not?'

'Yes, of course,' he says, with an indignant tone. 'But the concept of Senātus Populusque Rōmānus – the Senate and People of Rome being one – still held sway in 44 and the people still, mistakenly, saw themselves as a free citizenry. Openly dissolving the Senate by decree could have been seen as a step too far, a step we didn't want to risk, given the volatile nature of the Roman street. So, the final option we settled on was to provoke an outrage by the Senate. An outrage so egregious that the people would back abolishment of the Senate, if not clamour for it themselves. We discussed a number of scenarios to achieve this. Mark Antony came up with the boldest idea that we eventually agreed upon, even though it was risky, very risky.'

'And what was that?' I ask, digesting the implications of what I'm hearing.

'To engineer a plot against my own life. A plot that was so outrageous it would provoke popular anger and provide an undeniable justification to abolish the Senate.'

I sit bolt upright, cocking my head to one side, taken aback at what I've just heard. If I understand correctly, Caesar has just told me he's the mastermind behind the plot against his own life! If so, then this completely turns history on its head! My mind is now racing, as is my pulse.

'So, what went wrong?' I almost blurt.

'I knew there was a lot of risk, of course I did,' he replies with a sense of acceptance. 'But it was more important we achieved maximum impact and besides, the strategy was actually quite simple. Mark Antony took on the role of agent provocateur, inciting a small group of hostile senators to plot against me, and in turn, they drew other less committed senators in, until the plot grew and gained its own momentum. Mark Antony only had to pull the strings of the few ring leaders, and then they did the rest. He executed his task with brilliance.'

'So, who were these select few?'

'Decimus Brutus, Cassius Longinus and Tillius Cimber.'

'And not Marcus Junius Brutus?' I ask surprised, given he eventually delivered the "unkindest cut of all."

'No. As I said before, he was ambivalent until nearly the end,' Caesar replies, with an almost parental defensiveness. 'The momentum continued to build in the early months of 44 to the point where the plotters took the reins into their own hands and Mark Antony only had to keep a watchful eye on them. We therefore knew as soon as the date was set: March the fifteenth, the Ides of March. In the meantime, we'd been secretly infiltrating hand-picked veterans into Rome, those who'd served with us in the civil war, to take over the Senate once the assassination attempt failed.'

Caesar pauses, running his fingers through his badly thinning hair. 'So, to your point, my apparent lack of concern for my own safety and my comments welcoming death and so on, they were all just a ruse, intended to encourage the plotters. The priests were bribed by Mark Antony to provide the plotters with signs that the gods were against me and with them. Even on the morning of the assassination, I made a show of finally paying heed to the concocted warnings, by staying at home, at the insistence of Calpurnia, in order to egg on the plotters.'

'And what about your health problems, were they faked too?'

'My so-called morbid state of mind and what you call my

"death wish" were pure theatre, all part of an act to convince the plotters that I was vulnerable. Yes, it's true that I suffered from epilepsy, and not cerebrovascular disease as you posit, but you need to understand that epilepsy was viewed differently in ancient times; it was considered a divine disease and sufferers were seen to be touched by the gods. So it was actually a boon for my public image. In fact, I was extremely fit and healthy well into my fifties and was about to embark on a campaign against the Parthian Empire, not something a man suffering from heart disease would do, I can assure you,' he asserts with pride, knowing that he shamed soldiers thirty years his younger by his physical prowess and stamina in the field.

'But what about your father and great uncle's heart attacks?' I ask, uncertain.

'Maybe they were cardiac arrests. Maybe they were epileptic induced fatal seizures. Maybe they were something else, who knows. Autopsies were rare in those days,' he says with indifference.

'So back to my question then. What went wrong because, erm, well, you died, right?' This is awkward.

Caesar doesn't flinch. 'We had the plotters exactly where we wanted them. They had fallen for the bait, hook, line and sinker. Their planned attack at Pompey's theatre, where the senate was temporarily sitting that day, was exactly the outrage we'd hoped for – in plain daylight, with plenty of witnesses. It would entirely vindicate the abolition of the Senate and silence any doubters. The signal for the attack was to be Cimber, that rascal, pushing yet another petition on me, at which point the other plotters would crowd in brandishing their blades. But before they could do me any harm, Mark Antony was to rush in, grab Cimber and cry foul. Our veterans, who were in civilian clothing waiting in the wings of the porticus, would then charge in and disarm the plotters, exposing their blades for all to see. We even expected – I should say hoped for – a bit of bloodshed that would have lent drama to the whole thing.'

'But something went wrong,' I mutter, astounded by the

audacity of the plan.

'Hmm, something went wrong indeed,' Caesar echoes, with a sombre face. 'I let Decimus take me to the theatre as planned. We entered through the front and walked along the portico to the curia, and it was then that I suddenly sensed something was not quite right – call it a sixth sense, or soldier's intuition. My hackles were up. It felt like an ambush, a feeling I'd experienced many times before on campaign. So I had to make a split-second decision: follow my instincts, turn around and get out of there *and* destroy months of careful planning, or go through with it and trust my fortune. I trusted my fortune.'

'Why?' I ask, puzzled that he'd take such an enormous bet against his instincts.

'I rationalized that it felt like an ambush because it *was* an ambush.'

'What do you mean?'

'We knew the plotters would try to ambush me in the curia, before we in turn ambushed them – that was the plan. So of course the whole thing whiffed of an ambush! I walked to the end of the portico, just before it connects with the curia, with Decimus still trying to distract me with his prattling. I could see Cimber coming towards me at pace with the rest of the plotters closely at his back. It took all my years of experience and training to remain calm, in fact, looking back on it, the whole situation was surreal. I mean, how many people knowingly walk into their death like that?'

He shakes his head and sighs. 'Anyhow, I kept going forward, with Casca now upon me and I remember thinking: "where in the name of all the gods is Mark Antony? Why isn't he here ready to cry foul?" Casca flourished his petition in my face before reaching inside his toga for his blade and then it hit me! My stomach sank, my knees felt weak! I knew something had gone horribly wrong and it was too late. I had wittingly put my head in the noose and the trap door was about to open. Oddly enough though,' he pauses, looking suddenly reflective, 'I didn't feel any fear of death at that moment – many people have asked me that, but I've never feared death. Maybe that's why I was always so successful on the battlefield.

'Do you know what? I actually felt fury. I was furious with myself, furious that I'd put myself in that position, literally handing myself on a platter to my enemies. And then the first blow came. From Casca. Then the second, the third and then all of them – all twenty-three! And there was little I could do, other than protect my dignity by throwing my toga over my face. I was hopelessly outnumbered and unarmed.' Caesar lets out an ironic laugh, tinged with regret and bitterness. 'Caesar laid low by a cohort of panting, sweaty senators, something a thousand barbarian swords couldn't achieve,' he harrumphs. 'Farcical really.'

'So where was Mark Antony?' I ask, puzzled.

'Mark Antony, hmmm. Where was he indeed? Well, he wasn't where he was supposed to be, that's for sure,' Caesar says sarcastically, exhaling loudly. 'Mark Antony a few hours earlier had given the veterans new orders, unbeknownst to me at the time, to assemble at a meeting point outside the city walls, on the far side of the Campus Martius. There, he had them ambushed and their bodies dumped in the Tiber. As I was entering the theatre, Mark Antony allowed himself to be detained by one of the plotters, Gaius Trebonius I think, whose job it was to keep him away from me.'

'Mark Antony!' I exclaim, boggled. 'He set you up and allowed you to walk into a trap?' I stammer. I can hardly believe it. The drunk and debauched but unstintingly loyal Caesarian lieutenant actually betrayed his friend and master, through an elaborate double cross of Machiavellian proportions?

'Yes,' he sighs. 'It's all so obvious now. The signs were there. They were there for several years, but I missed them in my own, dare I say, blinkered pursuit of power, while all along it was Mark Antony that craved the ultimate power. He used me like a blind fool, so he could seize control of Rome. In hindsight it was brilliant, I have to admit, a plot within a plot within a plot and with all traces of his involvement buried forever with my death. My assassination would give him the loyalty of my legions and the sympathy of the people, positioning him as my natural successor and the new Dictator, or maybe even a king.

'Upon my death, he seized the state treasury and marched six thousand troops into Rome under Lepidus, to consolidate his position and was given custody of my estate and personal papers by Calpurnia. He had won. Rome and the world were at his feet, while I was a corpse under a bloody sheet.'

He pauses, downcast, running his fingers through his hair. And then out of the blue he does it again, dropping another history-shattering bombshell! 'And then there was Cleopatra of course,' he says mildly.

'Cleopatra?' I ask surprised. 'What did she have to do with this?'

'He was jealous. He'd fallen in love, madly in love, with her while she was staying in Rome. Of course, I noticed the flirting and all of that but thought nothing of it. In fact, I suppose I was flattered that he and every other man in Rome desired what only I had. Yes, I was blinded by my arrogance, I suppose,' he says reflectively. 'I failed to see the depth of his desire for her and probably hers for him, too. While I was alive, he could never have her, but with me dead, she was his.'

'So he betrayed you for love *and* power.'

'Isn't that always the way?' he says wryly. He sits up in his chair, straightening his back and looks me in the eye, a smile spreading across his face. 'But I had the last laugh, even in death,' he says enigmatically.

'The last laugh?' I repeat.

'Yes, I hid something from him, from everyone in fact, something he completely missed and would prove to be his undoing – and Cleopatra's.'

'What was that?' The twists and turns of this plot are making me giddy.

'Octavius, my great nephew. In my will I posthumously named Octavius as my legally adopted son and heir. Mark Antony literally fell off his chair, no doubt drunk again' – he says with a mixture of scorn and sarcasm – 'during the public reading of my will, when he heard that. He was left with a dilemma: either recognise Octavius as my successor and in so doing relinquish his own ambitions to succeed me or fight him. In the end he chose to fight, but never being the most astute of politicians, his support ebbed away and in time the people, and the legions sided with Octavius, who eventually defeated him and Cleopatra in battle at Actium, some thirteen years later. With his subsequent suicide in Egypt, the failure of his plot against me was complete. You could say I was avenged,' he says with melancholy.

'But his death didn't give me any satisfaction, as strange as that sounds. After all, he'd been my brother in arms and served me with unswerving loyalty for most of his life, in fact almost until the end. There'd also been too many deaths, too much bloodshed. Too many good men had fallen. And all for what?' Caesar stares into the distance, almost unaware of my presence, a look of deep sadness etched on his face.

'So, would you change anything? Would you do anything differently if you had your time over again, with the benefit of hindsight I mean?' I ask, drawing him back to the present.

He fixes me with his jet-black eyes, that seem to have now lost their lustre and states heavily 'You can't change history, history can only change you.'

'Es Tu Marcus Antonius. So Rest Caesar,' I half whisper to myself.

A CONVERSATION WITH CONSTANTINE XI DRAGAS PALEOLOGOS, THE LAST OF THE ROMANS

'So, why did you do it?'

Constantine contemplates the question, his brow furrowed, before slowly responding. 'I was dead anyway. I was dead the moment I was born. In fact, I was dead even before that. I was dead as far back as 1071,' he replies dismally, shifting uneasily in his chair, avoiding my gaze.

'I don't understand. You died on the night of 29th May 1453, right?' I state puzzled, checking my notes.

'That's correct – at least that's the day my corporeal self was cut down defending the breach, and my soul ascended to heaven. But the 26th August 1071 is the day the end of history commenced, the day my death was conceived. I suppose you could call it prospective in vitro mortis,' he says with a weary fatalism, his dark eyes shifting from side to side.

'The future can be written so far in the past? That's nearly four hundred years before your *bodily* death?' I reply, confused by his time twisting, wondering how he could have "died" some nearly three-hundred years before he was born.

'I suppose it can. Our ancestors cast the die for us, just as we cast the die for those we beget and those that they beget and so on,' he replies flatly.

'That sounds very fatalistic. If I understand you correctly, you're saying self-determination plays no part in shaping our lives, that we're simply pushed along on history's currents, rudderless, with no ability to chart our own course.'

'You can't control the cards you're dealt with, but you may decide how you play those cards, so it's a combination of predetermination and self-determination,' he clarifies.

'I see, so you had nothing to lose that night in 1453 by plunging into the breach, throwing yourself into certain death, because your whole life was leading up to that point?'

'I had everything to lose by *not* plunging into the breach that night, my honour, my faith, my duty to my people, my allegiance to my soldiers, and my love for my country. To do otherwise would have been to stain for posterity the name of Constantinople and the dignity of our ancestors – I was after all the last of our kind, carrying the torch for an ancient civilization, one that went back thousands of years to the very founding of Rome.'

'That sounds like a heavy burden to carry.'

'Yes, but lightened by my faith,' he replies, the shine of the true believer in his eyes.

'You've mentioned your faith several times, obviously faith is very important to you, but was your faith in your God rewarded on that night? I mean, you and your people essentially died in a bloodbath, didn't you? A horrific massacre with women and children slain in the streets, your holy sites torched and desecrated and all this despite desperate supplications to your God, and not to mention a millennia of devout religious observation before that,' I challenge him.

'You can't question the way of the Father,' he replies calmly. 'If you try to interpret events – especially momentous events such as those on the 25th of May 1453 – through a clinical eye, you'll always fail to see the divine at work and instead just find self-serving excuses that point to the absence of God. Faith is not about questioning; faith is about believing. God works in mysterious ways, ways that are beyond the understanding of man,' he states with conviction. 'Let me tell you, as we were preparing for the abandonment of the last toehold of the true faith in the East, that faith was moving inexorably westwards, across the oceans, to find new and fertile lands in the Americas. It's hard to understand his grand designs when you choose only to see one piece of the picture.'

'But was it not your cynical attitude to the true faith – many would say your heretical decision to endorse the unification of the Western and Eastern churches at the Council of Florence in 1431 – the true reason God abandoned you and your people? Did not your own Megas Doux, Loukas Notaras, vehemently state: "Better to see the turban of the Infidel bobbing in the Church of the Holy Wisdom than the Latin mitre!" And George Sphrantzes, a contemporary chronicler pointed out that, and I quote: "the Church of God is the Church of the East and the Church of the East is Constantinople, all being indivisible and divine. Whosoever abandons that divinity shall cause God to abandon Constantinople and cause the flag of the Infidel to fly from its tallest spires."

'After all the true faith, the Orthodoxy and the holy relics, including the one and true cross and the crown of thorns, were entrusted by God to you through your office as the spiritual leader of the Eastern Church. The empire had faced impossible odds in the past and had always triumphed by holding true to the Orthodox faith, defeating countless enemies and regaining conquered territory time after time. Is it no wonder, therefore, that God was a little upset that you endorsed a Council that supinely recognised the universal and supreme jurisdiction of the Bishop of Rome over the Eastern Church. Was this not surely an abrogation of the holy pact between you and God?' I challenge him.

Constantine glares at me, clearly unimpressed with my rendering of the schism between the Catholic and Orthodox faiths. 'You're employing selective facts and quotes to build a case that is fallacious, at best,' he replies testily. 'Would God really care about the turgid circular debate between the theologians of Constantinople and Rome? The schism was so esoteric as to be self-indulgent and fanciful, nothing more than endless hand wringing over the meaning of purgatory; the definition and number of the sacraments; whether the Holy Ghost should be included in the Trinity; and whether a word should be inserted here or there in the Nicene-Constantinopolitan Creed. Such dogma is the province of man, not God. Besides, my endorsement of the Laetentur Caeli, the final decree of union, was essentially an act of diplomacy, an act designed to garner support from the Papal forces for the coming conflict with Islam.'

'But military assistance never came, did it? Other than a handful of Genoese and Venetian adventurers,' I scoff. 'Another sign perhaps of God's dissatisfaction with the subjugation of the Eastern Church?'

'That assistance would have come, was coming, in fact...' he suddenly stops mid-sentence, as if unsure of himself.

Odd, I think to myself, but I ignore it and continue.

'Surely the signs of God's displeasure could not have been any more obvious than the portents visited upon Constantinople in the days leading up to the Ottoman siege in 1453,' I state picking up my notes. 'George Sphrantzes noted in alarm that: "at midday the moon obscured the sun and all became dark as if it were the depths of the night. Then appeared a ghostly blood red ring that circled and soon enveloped the dome of the Church of the Holy Wisdom," and: "they took the most revered holy icons onto the Augusteum including our Lady Virgin and made a procession through the streets, seeking holy intercession to save the city but the Virgin tumbled and fell to the ground, to which they proceeded to place her back, for her to only fall a second time, much to the consternation and alarm of the people who took it as the darkest of omens." The prominent Byzantine Michael Ducas wrote: "Suddenly thunder shook the very foundations of the city and a great deluge, the likes of which had not been seen in our lifetime, rained down upon us, causing flood everywhere as if the very canals of Venice had poured into the streets," and that was in May, a month not known for its precipitation,' I add.

Constantine looks somewhat vexed, his powerful jawline tensing. 'They were strange days, no doubt, but we were living in strange times. What can I say?' he says resignedly with a shrug of his broad shoulders.

'Okay, well let's go back to that night on the ramparts,' I reply, taking the conversation away from the theological and back to the day he died defending the city walls. 'Was there no hope at all, no hope of escape, no possibility of surrender, or even negotiation? Was death really the only option for you?'

Constantine sighs, contemplating me. 'You have to understand the situation was desperate. We'd sustained heavy bombardment for weeks, the walls were crumbling beneath us, and the men were exhausted. Day after day in an endless cycle, we'd repel wave after wave of Ottoman troops in the hours of light and then under cover of darkness repair the breaches in the walls, brick by brick. After two months of siege, there was barely any food in the city; we'd resorted to eating rats and domestic animals, cats, dogs, anything that could be skinned and roasted.'

I wince at the thought, and he notices.

'Dog tastes better than cat,' he adds for my obvious benefit. 'On the 29th, in the morning, an unholy din picked up from outside the walls, coming from the enemy's camp; cymbals, horns, drums, the clarion calls of war – it was deafening and unnerving. I knew what was coming, I knew that sound. I'd heard it since I was a child, a constant companion ringing in my head, nagging at me, taunting me as the last of my line. It was the death knell, the end of history, the end of everything, echoing down through the ages since 1071,' he pauses momentarily, biting down on his lower lip. 'I immediately ordered every bell in the city to ring in defiance, to show the enemy that God was with us, and we were ready – God willing – to fight and die for our faith and for our families. And then they came.' Constantine pauses again, looking into the middle distance, his brown eyes, set deep in his solid skull, glazed and slightly rheumy.

'"Then they came,"' I prompt him.

'The horsemen of the apocalypse came and with them all the hosts of hell, wave after unstoppable wave, blotting out the horizon. The very earth shook, the walls and ramparts trembled, men lost their footing, the air was filled with grit and dust and cries – it was like the Devil had smashed his fist into the ground and shaken the earth. We were in shock before eventually came to our senses and rained volley after volley down upon them from the ramparts, with guns and crossbow. Yet they had no care; they ran up to the walls, not afraid of death, each one wanting to be the first to fly their Prophet's flag from the towers and win their place in Paradise. How can you defeat such a foe that embraces death like that?'

Constantine looks shell-shocked, shaking his head from side to side, his voice unsteady. 'Then came a final volley of fire from their bombards, a withering hail of death that blackened the sky, tearing through the ramparts, like a storm from hell. Thick clouds of acrid smoke covered the walls and the fields beyond, shrouding our field of vision. And then a heavy silence fell, for maybe a minute or so, an eerie silence, the calm before the storm, I guess, broken by a soft rumbling that grew into a mighty crescendo. Their war cry pierced the fog before we saw them; the Janissaries – the elite of the Ottoman soldiers and the Sultan's favourites – dashed over a sea of their fallen, until they got to the walls and raised their scaling ladders.

'As fast we could push them down, a replacement came and another and another. We were vastly outnumbered, but we fought like madmen, like men who had nothing to lose – apart from the judgment of history.'

'Was it at this point that Giovanni Giustiniani was grievously wounded?' I ask, referring to the commander of the Genoese volunteers who was pivotal in the defence of the city.

'He was close by, leading the defence of the Mesoteichion – the middle section of the land walls – when a projectile struck him, piercing his breastplate. I remember seeing him clutching at his chest, screaming in pain as he fell to the floor. His men picked him up and started to carry him off, but I ordered him to stay and fight to the end. He could still stand just, and I believe he could have carried on fighting. And I knew if he abandoned the walls, it would crush morale along the Genoese lines, and that's exactly what happened; the sight of their general being carried off caused the Genoese to believe the battle was lost, and to a man they turned tail and fled to their ships in the Golden Horn. With the Genoese out of the battle, there was little hope left. The Janissaries soon overwhelmed the Mesoteichion, and the walls were breached.'

'Were you bitter that the Genoese abandoned their positions?' I ask, curious.

'There was no time for recriminations. In hindsight the Genoese fought bravely, they were under no obligation to be there, they could have left weeks before. They were foreign volunteers and until that moment had stood shoulder to shoulder with us. Besides, Giustiniani was a brilliant general and was vastly more experienced in siege warfare than we were, so to be frank, we couldn't have lasted as long as we did without him. Would I have done the same if Genoa was under siege? A Latin city on the wrong side of the Schism? I don't know. I can only be grateful for their help, laying down their lives for us, as Giustiniani eventually did.'

'So, with the Genoese out of the fray, I guess your own death was, erm, fairly imminent?' I ask.

'A small postern gate, the Kerkoporta, had been left open by saboteurs and the Janissaries flooded through, raising their flags on the tower. Panic ensued once the men saw the infidel flags flying; it took grip of them and fanned out across the ramparts like wildfire – men who had only moments before been staring down the enemy and smiting them with the courage of Angels, turned tail and fled. Many of them ran to their homes to be with their families in the final hours. There was no more that could be done, nothing, we'd given everything and had now lost everything. I knew what to do. I'd rehearsed it in my mind for weeks, if not months, maybe even years,' he states, straightening his large frame in the seat that barely holds him, his chest – encased in a breastplate sporting the imperial eagle – pushed forward, as if preparing for battle once more.

'Maybe since 1071?' I suggest wryly.

'Yes, maybe,' he says, creasing his forehead, mulling it over for a few seconds. 'I was not going to be captured by the Ottomans. I was not going to suffer the indignity of being paraded through the streets, bound and dragged behind Mehmed's horse, only to have my head skewered on a stake and make a meal for the crows,' he states wearing a dark look. 'I swore upon the Holy Cross that Romanos IV would be the only Emperor ever to be taken alive by the Ottomans. I threw off my royal cloak and any other visible trappings of rank and jumped off the ramparts into the chaos below.

'The Janissaries were by now flooding into the city, chopping down everyone in their path. I rushed into their midst with a few men, cutting and thrusting, lashing out all around us, until the inevitable, until I was overwhelmed. And then...' Constantine pauses suddenly, struggling to form words. He stares at me, cold and grey, a look of total mystification on his face, as if he can't fathom what happened next.

After a few moments I continue the story for him: '"...at the moment of his death the Arch Angel himself descended to him, spreading his wings and gently lifting him, bearing him up to heaven," so recounts Nicolò Barbaro, the Venetian surgeon, who witnessed your death. And Barbaro continues: "the Emperor looked down upon his city and wept."'

Constantine shuts his eyes, his mighty head sagging, no doubt recalling the moments of his ascension, as he looked down helplessly upon his people and his city in shock, as he abandoned them forever.

'What of your people? What happened to them once the line was broken and the Ottomans flooded into the city?' I ask mildly.

'Savagery and madness swept through the city. No one was spared, nowhere was safe. The elderly, the women and children, all put to the sword – or worse. The streets ran with blood, torrents of crimson that were so thick that you slid in it. People fled their homes, blindly huddling together in the streets, out of their minds with terror. You can't begin to understand what such fear feels like,' he exclaims, visibly shaking as he recounts the horrors.

'It's as if you're trapped in your own worst nightmare but without ever waking up. Many sort sanctuary in the Church of the Holy Wisdom. Thousands flooded in, but many people were left outside to their fate when the great doors were finally barred. Inside was a scene of utter despair, mothers clung to their children, priests desperately prayed for last minute salvation, a few soldiers desperately tried to hold the doors. But it wasn't long before the Ottomans smashed through, a surge of madness sweeping everyone before it. They cut down the old and infirm where they stood, despite their desperate pleas for mercy; they dragged screaming children away from their parents, smashing their heads against the ground before raping their mothers; nuns were ripped away bare breasted clinging to the altar and suffered indignities that I cannot speak of; and the holy relics, they were snatched up and tossed into the flames. Those who were left alive were carried off in chains to be sold as slaves or kept as playthings to satisfy the debased appetites of the Sultan's soldiers. And so, it carried on, throughout all the churches and places of sanctuary, for three whole days and nights.'

'"It was the last night after a thousand years, it was the first night of a thousand tears,"' I quote George Sphrantzes softly.

'It was the end of history, the end of civilization, all gone, utterly destroyed,' he replies ashen faced. 'Since Constantine the Great founded our city in 330 AD, we were the torch bearers of the Roman Empire. We were the inheritors of the Graeco-Roman world, the guardians of the very scrolls of Plato and Aristotle, transported from the great library of Alexandria. We were the shining light of philosophy, art, science, and literature when that light was snuffed out in the Dark Ages. A thousand years destroyed in one night of madness, tossed onto a bonfire of malice and spite, a funeral pyre for the Roman world. Never has there been such vandalism of an entire history, people, and culture as happened that day,' he laments, shell shocked.

'Yet, it was you that lit that fire, was it not?' I state, looking him straight in the eye, my own cold and hard. Constantine stares back at me with a sudden look of alarm and bewilderment, reeling from my unexpected accusation.

'What do you mean?' he stammers, confusion and indignation in his voice.

'The obsession with 1071. The sense of manifest destiny ringing in your head since you were a boy. The fatalistic belief that you were ordained to die the tragic hero, a martyr's death. All classic symptoms of a form of psychosis called delusional disorder. This delusion prevented you from considering any other options apart from a hopeless fight to the bitter end – let me quote Loucas Notaras: "The Emperor was implacable in his opposition to discussion of any plans that did not end in a heroic last stand, despite our pleas to the contrary." And there were acceptable alternatives to your death and devastation of your city. As late as the 21st of May, only eight days before Constantinople fell, Mehmed sent an ambassador to you offering to lift the siege if you surrendered. He also promised to allow you and anyone else to leave with all their possessions, unharmed. Moreover, he would recognise you as governor of the Peloponnese and guarantee the safety of those that chose to remain behind in Constantinople, and without the requirement to convert to Islam, I may add. And what did you do? You flatly rejected these generous face-saving terms, with the blase reply: "as to surrendering the city to you, it is not for me to decide, or for anyone of us, for all of us have reached the decision to die as free men."

'It was you that had no regard for the lives of your subjects; they were merely sacrificial lambs on the altar of your delusion. Again, I quote Notaras: "when it was heard the terms the Sultan of the Ottomans had offered and that our Emperor had rejected, there was consternation and dismay amongst the populace, for they wished more for life under the Crescent than death on the Cross." From the Ottoman side there was incredulity too: "he has set himself against life and seeks only death for his own glory; it can now only be our sacred duty to oblige him," stated Mehmed's Vizier, Halil Pasha, upon hearing the news of your rejection. Even the indefatigable Giustiniani counselled you to consider saving yourself and the city: “my Lord, ‘tis not for a Latin tongue to sway the Emperor of the Romans – for my home is beyond the reach of the Ottoman guns – but think of the innocents who will die here,” noted Barbaro in his diary. Therefore, I contend it was you, and you alone, who consigned Constantinople to the flames and her people to the sword. You who have the blood of thirty thousand people staining your hands, you who subjected the women and boys to the basest of sexual depredations!’

And to drive home the point, I strike an emotional blow, borrowing from Barbaro’s diary again: “I saw a woman scream out in terror as an Ottoman soldier violated her in the most unspeakable manner and then tossed her to his comrade to repeat the same debased act – I cannot but fear that this sight was oft repeated throughout the night.”’

‘You have no idea what you’re talking about!’ Constantine responds in a raised voice, almost yelling at me, clenching and unclenching his fists.

‘Don’t I? Let’s go back to the summer of 1444, then, shall we – when you were the ruler of the Despotate of the Morea in modern day Greece. You struck northwards, invading the Duchy of Athens, forcing its Florentine duke, Nerio II Acciaioli, a vassal of the Sultan, to pay you tribute, a move that only had one possible outcome and that was to provoke a devastating Ottoman response – a response that you would have known full well would come. According to the Byzantine chronicler, Laonikos Chalkokondyles, this was the rashest of strategic moves, utterly confounding your contemporaries. “Why provoke the Sultan like this; better to put your head in the mouth of a lion and pray to God the beast has no appetite,” wrote Chalkokondyles.’

‘Chalkokondyles, what did he know?’ Constantine scoffs, glaring at me, a slightly wild look on his face.

‘The Sultan, Murad II, led an army of fifty thousand men into Greece to put a swift end to your provocation,’ I continue. ‘In November the Ottomans reached the strongest of your defences, the Hexamilion wall, and by December, the Janissaries had smashed through thanks to their bombards, and you barely escaped with your life. Does this not sound like an eerie forerunner to the siege of Constantinople and the breakthrough in the Mesoteichion walls that led to your 'heroic' demise? Again, it was the ordinary people, your people, that paid the price for your deluded actions: the Morea was devastated, and sixty thousand people were taken prisoner and sold into slavery, while you and your brother were forced to become vassals of Murad.

'Ironically, while you couldn't fulfil your "destiny" that time around, this self-inflicted defeat laid the foundations for the destruction of Constantinople itself. The young Mehmed – who accompanied his father Murad on the campaign – swore never to allow the Christians to be in a position to challenge Ottoman rule again: "To prevent the insults of the Romans, is to once and for all conquer Constantinople," he's recorded saying to Zagan Pasha. In other words, you irrevocably hardened his position against Constantinople, a position that was not inevitable given the restraint his more moderate advisors, such as Halil Pasha, had on him. But your attack on Athens played straight into the hands of the hardliners, like Zagan, who could now pull the young Mehmed into their sway...the drumbeats of destiny, ringing in your head, dare I say.'

Constantine contemplates me with hollow, red-rimmed eyes. Suddenly, he starts laughing – a cold, mirthless laugh right in my face.

'I'd seen the attack on Constantinople coming for several years; it wasn't hard to foresee! Mehmed was not his father, not the careful calculating statesman who had sought expansion in Europe while avoiding provoking the Latin kingdoms into a united campaign against him. No, Mehmed was a young man in a hurry, a hurry to make his own mark on history and distance himself from his father. Besides, he suffered from a fiercely aggressive temper and couldn't be reasoned with, as several headless emissaries attested to. When he started construction on a second fortress on the Bosporus, barely ten miles north of

Constantinople, any doubts about his intentions were dispelled – not that *I* ever had any,' he adds to make a point.

'That was why we'd been planning for years, carefully laying the foundations of a master plan, a plan that would once and for all push the Ottomans east of the Bosporus and secure Constantinople's future forever.'

'Master plan? What master plan?' I scoff, recalling there was no mention of a "master plan" in any of the research I undertook over several months in preparation for this discussion.

'I'd been cultivating relationships with the Venetians for over a decade,' he replies calmly. 'They were wily and suspicious and had to be handled patiently, and in 1450, I sent my half-brother Andronikos on a mission to the court of the Doge, Francesco Foscari, to bring matters to a head.'

'Venetians?' I ask incredulously.

'Yes. The Venetians were vital to this master plan,' Constantine replies firmly. 'They had the largest naval yard in the world, the Arsenale di Venezia, and could lay one hull a day, on a production line that no one else could rival – certainly not the Ottomans, with their ships that were little more than rowing boats and took months to construct,' he scoffs. 'We knew that if we offered the Venetians *certain* inducements, they could outfit at least three hundred ships in our service, some from their own fleet, and be ready to sail to Constantinople in less than six months. We planned to have one hundred of the most manoeuvrable vessels, the galiots, and fustas, sail up the Bosporus and cut the Ottoman supply lines between Europe and Asia, as well as destroy the Sultan's navy in the process. A few of the heavier galeas were to sail further north up the Bosporus, and pound the Ottoman throat cutter forts of Rumelihisarı and Anadoluhisarı, as well as block the Straits, in the event the Genoese colonies on the Black Sea decided to send ships to support the Ottomans. The remaining ships were to be split into two flotillas; one would board troops in the southern Morea under the command of my brothers, Thomas and Demetrios and land reinforcements just south of Constantinople, circumventing the Ottoman's land blockade. The remaining flotilla was to harass the Ottomans, along the Dardanelles, to distract their forces and tie up their coastal garrisons.'

'That sounds like an extraordinary risk for the Venetians to take,' I remark, sceptically. 'In essence, it would have been a *casus belli* for outright war with the Ottoman Empire – a conflict they had meticulously avoided for the past century. After all, to the ever-pragmatic Venetians, war was detrimental to business.'

'Your comments are fair but only up to a point. The fall of Thessaloniki some ten years earlier, as the fall of Nicopolis before it, was a rude awakening for the Venetians. The fitful peace that prevailed with the Ottomans was being upended by the relative ease, with which they could now conquer and hold territory in the Balkans and further west. A faction within Venice, "La Fazione," led by Micheletto Attendolo and Piero Priuli, feared the loss of their Aegean territories to an ascendant Ottoman empire, with the potential end game being an attack via the Peloponnese on Italy and Venice itself. To prevent this nightmare scenario, they formulated a policy of forward defence, attacking and pushing back the Ottomans on the fringes of their eastern Mediterranean possessions. We in Constantinople, of course, carefully nurtured and funded La Fazione, even hinting at a joint alliance against the Ottomans.'

'Having a faction of radicals on your side is one thing, but securing the backing of the Doge and the Council of Ten is an entirely different matter,' I protest.

Constantine shoots me an impatient glance before continuing.

'There was a sure-fire way to get under the Doge's skin: the Genoese. He despised them, and it wasn't just about the rivalry for control of Mediterranean trade. He had a personal vendetta against Pietro di Campofregoso, the ruler of Genoa. The Doge couldn't stand him, and for good reason, I suppose – Campofregoso had the Doge's cousin executed and then, allegedly, raped his widow,' he shrugs and carries on. 'So, it wasn't difficult to devise a proposition to entice the Doge. Essentially, we proposed to expel the Genoese from Constantinople and the Bosphorus, revoke all their trading rights, and grant Venice a trading monopoly between East and West. We presented this idea first to Priuli, who immediately recognised the opportunity – combining trade and forward defence in one stroke.

'He then took it to the Doge, whose ear he had, given his roles as state treasurer and an avogadoria de comun. Even then, the agreement wasn't sealed, and we had to offer additional concessions—territory in the Morea—to secure the support of the entire Council of Ten.'

For the first time, I see a glimmer of satisfaction -- a recognition of a job well done – cross his otherwise morose face. Indeed, he had devised a stunning plan of boldness and cunning, a Byzantine effort of diplomacy, if he could be believed.

Suddenly, he bursts out: 'Can you now see why I didn't consider surrender? Why I aimed for victory? My actions were not those of a deluded man but of someone with strategic clarity. Right up to the twenty-seventh of May, I expected the fleet to enter the Marmara and break the siege. Every action I took was designed to buy extra time for those ships. Right up to the last hour, I was not prepared to abandon hope and surrender years of manoeuvring and planning.'

He stares at me, animated, seeking my understanding and his vindication, but there is still one obvious flaw in this story:

'But what about the ships? We know the three hundred ships never made it to the Bosphorus. Maybe twelve at best sailed into Constantinople, and there was no Venetian intervention to save the day. So, what happened? How did the plan unravel? Why did Constantinople fall despite all your prodigious efforts?' I challenge him.

Constantine draws a deep breath and lets out a sigh, his countenance returning to its usual glum state. 'Everyone had sworn to the utmost secrecy – we couldn't let the Ottomans learn of our plans and risk them bringing forward the attack on Constantinople. The Venetians didn't even put it to a vote in their Senate for this reason, and outside of my brothers and a few other trusted advisors, no one else knew about our plans. Things started out well; we made payments and building commenced and in the early summer of 1452 ships were even floated in the lagoons – I really believed the plan was coming to pass.'

He makes a sucking noise and shakes his head, before continuing. 'But then, towards the end of summer, things started to unravel, just small things at first but soon followed by more serious mishaps: a fire that sent a dozen ships to the bottom; an outbreak of plague in the shipyards; delays in timber and canvas arriving; and ominously, long lapses in dispatches from Andronikus in Venice. By mid-autumn I was starting to worry. We knew the Ottomans would start campaigning in early spring the following year, and I hadn't heard from Andronikus since late summer. I was ready to set out for Venice myself to find out what was going on, but I was dissuaded by my council and sent personal emissaries instead.

'A few weeks after their departure, letters came back from the Venetians, both from the Doge and also from Piruli, whom I trusted much more. They were full of filial regards and assurances that all was now well after some initial setbacks and building would be sped up to ensure they met their commitments on time. But it wasn't convincing. Something was wrong. The tone was too floral and smelled of Venetian intriguing. And with the emissaries not having returned – a concern of itself – it was hard to fathom what was really going on. Still, I didn't give up hope, or faith, even then. Surely God was still with us,' he states, a mix of conviction and hope in his voice.

'God moves in mysterious ways…' I suggest, smiling.

He ignores my comment and continues. 'It's hardly believable. After all these years, I still can't take it in. It was the slimmest of misfortunes, the devil's own work.' He pauses, shaking his head from side to side, staring at the floor. 'Despite his vow of secrecy, the Doge had sent a message to his brother-in-law, Jacopo Mantegna, in the summer of 1452, warning him to depart Adrianople, where he was serving as Venetian ambassador to the Sultan's Court. As fate would have it, Mantegna was in

Constantinople at the time the letter arrived in Adrianople, and it was opened by his mistress, who was, of course, in the pay of the Grand Vizier.

'The Sultan couldn't believe his luck when he read the letter, outlining in detail the pact between Constantinople and Venice. To him, it was a sign from God, confirming his destiny to conquer Constantinople and inherit our empire. The Ottomans then quickly developed a counter plan that was as bold and cunning as the plan it was designed to thwart – I have to give them that much,' he states sullenly. 'The Ottomans set out to turn several notable men in my Court to their cause, including my nephews, Michael and Demetrious.'

I raise my eyebrows in surprise.

'Yes, my nephews harboured a deep seated animosity towards me, based on an unfounded belief that I was involved in their father's murder, and their animosity was only inflamed when my betrothal to the daughter of the King of Georgia was announced that year. They feared that any male offspring from our union would mean their disinheritance upon my death.

'The Sultan's web spread throughout Constantinople, his Grand Vizier had spies everywhere, and it wasn't hard for the Ottomans to rub salt into my nephews' wounds, inflaming their grievances and luring them with the promise of Michael, the eldest, becoming Emperor if they betrayed me. With this agreement, the brothers became pivotal in the Ottoman plans and Demetrious was dispatched to Venice to turn the Venetians against me with a counter proposal. The merchants of the lagoons, ever pliable and avaricious, now found themselves with a more compelling offer. The Ottomans offered them exclusive trading rights and the total expulsion of the Genoese from both Galata and the Black Sea, and importantly to the Venetians, a pact that would see them release pressure on Venetian possessions in the Aegean and a complete Ottoman pullback from Negroponte, Lemnos and Albania Veneta.

'The final part of the offer, however, was the most bitter and exemplified the treacherous nature of the Venetians,' Constantine states with disgust. 'They were given the rights of pre-plunder of Constantinople before it fell to the Ottomans. The right to desecrate and rob our holy places, as if our wealth and worth were some chattels to be bartered in the market between thieves. Even Piruli and La Fazione were eventually swayed, subordinating their long-term strategic concerns in deference to low risk returns from siding, rather than warring with the Ottomans. The Merchants of Venice, the perfidious republic,' he scoffs.

'And *did* they take their pound of flesh?' I ask.

'Under cover of the fighting, four Venetian merchantmen slipped out of Constantinople during the last days of the siege, their hulls lying low in the water with Constantinopolitan treasure, the holiest of our holy relics: the Crown of Thorns; the Shroud; and the one Cross, the true Cross. What became of these vestiges of Christ, I don't know. Maybe the Doge sold them on, and now, centuries later, they're gathering dust in a private collection in Geneva or New York, or maybe they were chopped up for firewood. Who knows.

'Anyhow, so all the "mishaps" I mentioned to you earlier, during the late summer of 1452, were all deliberate acts of sabotage designed to ensure the ships never set sail. Our fate was already sealed, unbeknownst to us at the time and the rest, well, you know...'

Constantine lowers his gaze, with a resigned shrug of his shoulders, while I, *me*, feel aggrieved on his behalf at the double crossing and intriguing – especially the family betrayal – that led to his downfall.

As if reading my mind, he raises his head slightly and says softly: 'But if you dance with the devil...the Venetians got their trading concessions, all right, but not at the expense of the Genoese. They stayed put in Galata and far from détente with the Ottomans, the Venetians lost every single one of their eastern Mediterranean possessions over the ensuing years. As for my nephews, well, not quite Emperors of Constantinople; Michael served as Governor of the Balkans and Demetrious became Admiral of the Ottoman fleet. But, I should add, Mehmed forced both of them to convert to Islam and suffer that "unkindest cut" that befalls all converts.'

Did I detect a hint of a smirk on his face?

I glance at the clock. There's one final matter to address, a shadow looming over our conversation from the start. Leaning forward, I fix him with a steady gaze. 'So, tell me, 1071. The year you died, only to be miraculously reborn four centuries later. What's the story behind that?'

Constantine smiles wearily in response. 'It's simple. There's no great mystery to it. On the twenty sixth of August, 1071, the Ottomans crushed the Byzantine army at Manzikert in modern day Turkey, capturing my ancestor, Emperor Romanos IV, which precipitated the slow but inexorable death of our Empire. That defeat robbed us of our lands in Anatolia and Armenia and opened the floodgates for a migration of Turkic peoples eastward into Asia minor and eventually across the Bosporus into Europe. Loss of land meant loss of taxes to fund armies, and loss of people meant loss of manpower to man armies. As I said, it was the day history ended, the day I died, the day the die was cast. By 1453 there was nothing left of the Empire apart from a rump state in the Morea, Constantinople itself and a few outposts in the Balkans. Hardly a heartland to hold back the Ottoman tide from.

'If the Byzantine-Venetian pact had played out, things would have been different, but it didn't and I guess history reasserted itself, as it always does,' he replies, heavy with melancholy. 'After his troops had sacked the city, Mehmed rode into the Augusteum, dismounted from his horse and kissed the ground. He then strode alone, overwhelmed by the moment I imagine, into the Boukoleon, the Palace of the Caesars and gazed around with insolent satisfaction. He'd finally fulfilled his destiny. And then...history ended, the end of time... the end of everything... all gone.'

A silence descends upon us. I can barely imagine how the twenty-one-year-old Sultan Mehmed II must have felt, as he sent his Muezzin to call the faithful to prayer for the first time from the highest reaches of the Church of the Holy Wisdom, the final conqueror of the Roman Empire, an empire that had stood for two thousand years. And then no more. I slowly pick up my notes then quote the famous words Mehmed uttered when he entered the Palace of the Caesars:

"'The spider is curtain-bearer in the palace of Chosroes,
The owl sounds the relief in the castle of Afrasiyab.'"

Constantine XI Dragas Paleologos, the last Emperor of the Romans, looks at me quizzically. He stares at me for a full minute before unexpectedly reciting the eulogy of Constantinople, penned by Cardinal Isidore of Kiev, a contemporaneous witness to Mehmed's triumph:

"'All is still, all silent, terror begets a terrible silence,
Only the carrion crow caw disturbs the desolate scene.
A thousand years washed away,
A few hours of violence, all gone, utterly gone,
The haughtiest civilization, now lowly desolation.
The dead echo haunts the Palace of the Caesars,
The blood red sun sets and weeps,
God has gone, God has come.'"

The poem's haunting beauty reflects in his face, its pathos causing his eyes to mist. A single lonely tear rolls down his cheek. I turn away and reflect upon the man in front of me. A man who tried to do his very best to serve his people, his country, his God. A man of deep conviction and belief. A man with a heightened sense of the burden of history – his history, his burden – but ultimately a flawed man, who caused his people to burn at the stake, sacrificing them in his blind determination to never cede an inch to his ancestral enemy.

His last known words, spoken in his mortal state, spring to my mind, words that while noble, were ultimately futile and self-serving, the words he spoke on the walls just as they were breached, spoken as a general, a comrade in arms, an Emperor honour bound to lead from the front:

"'I would not go if there was any benefit to leave the city, but I cannot go away...I will not leave, ever. I have decided to die with you.'"

A CONVERSATION WITH ALBERT EINSTEIN

'Why did you do it?' I ask.

'Mileva and I were young, and I suppose, naïve. We didn't really know what we were doing, we had no experience in these matters,' he states, looking reflective and slightly pained. 'You could even say we were...cowardly,' he continues, shoulders hunched, avoiding eye contact with me.

'Cowardly? Why would you say cowardly,' I ask, a little surprised.

'Because we bent to the social mores of the day, we allowed ourselves to be brow beaten by Mileva's parents, dragooned into doing the so called "right thing." We chose to abandon a young innocent life, our own daughter, to save ourselves the shame and moral opprobrium of acknowledging her as our own. I guess, we thought of our careers and our reputations first and foremost.' Einstein sighs heavily, his head bent, looking more dishevelled than usual. 'It's something I still feel ashamed about and a regret that haunted me for the rest of my life, a regret I carry beyond the grave to this day,' he states miserably, looking away.

'Do you know what happened to her? Did you ever try to trace her in later life?' I ask, assuming this is what I – most parents in fact – would have done in his shoes.

'No. Again something I bitterly regret. All I know was that Lieserl was adopted in 1902 in Novi Sad, Serbia – to whom I don't know. Mileva didn't like to talk about it, for obvious reasons, and I didn't want to drive a wedge between us, so I let it go; it was hard enough on her as it was.' He sighs again, looking lost in his oversized smoking jacket. 'But I suppose, to put it in some sort of context, it was 1902, and having a child out of wedlock was... well...seen as immoral, even wicked, given the social rigidities of the times. The pressure from Mileva's parents was intense; they were horrified at the shame of it, and Miloš, her father, was a dominating and hugely influential figure in her life. I can only imagine the immense burden she would have felt at the time.'

'Yet, you went on to have other children with Meliva didn't you – they must have given you some solace and joy?'

'Yes, well yes and no; sources of joy and sources of sadness. I guess if we're all brutally honest with ourselves, children always bring both in almost equal measure, don't they?' he muses, stroking his unkempt moustache.

'That sounds very *Newtonian*. What do you mean by that?' I quiz.

'I can't pretend I was ever the ideal father to any of my children. Poor old Tete, he spent most of his adulthood in and out of institutions. If I'd spent more time with him, paid more attention to his treatment, questioned his doctors, been his bedside advocate – he must have gone through a terrifying ordeal in that dark satanic place!' Einstein rubs his eyes. 'Mileva did her best; she was a good mother, no doubt about that, but her health was failing, and I should have been there more, much more.'

I study him for a moment and can't help wondering if this self-excoriation is somehow cathartic for him – maybe he's been bottling this up for a long time.

'You're referring to your son Eduard's – I mean Tete's – schizophrenia, I take it?'

'Yes, they treated him with electroconvulsive therapy, which in those days was little better than electrocution, frying a person's brain with a low voltage current. Where's the science in that?' he protests. 'I suppose there's always been a fine line between clinical advances that genuinely benefit the patient and experimentation to simply satisfy medical curiosity – especially when it comes to clinical psychiatry – a line that's too often crossed in my mind,' he states with some bitterness.

Images from "One Flew Over the Cuckoo's Nest" spring to

my mind, as I imagine poor old Tete strapped to a cold metal table, limbs flapping spastically, terror and confusion stamped in his eyes, as implacable men in white coats dial up the electric current that wracks his body.

'So, do you think if you'd cared for him more at home his clinical outcomes might have been different?'

'Possibly, it's hard to say, but at least I could have tried. But what I do know is the therapy hollowed him out, made him a husk of a man. The spark went out of him. I could see his deadened soul through his eyes, eyes that stared at you but didn't see you, that just looked into the distance.'

Einstein's own eyes, now dulled and red rimmed, seem to mirror a deep sense of guilt and regret that he wasn't fully there for his son.

'And you never saw him again after you emigrated to the States in 1933?'

He pauses, contemplative for a few moments, teasing his moustache. 'We corresponded for the rest of our lives. It was a great source of joy when I received his letters, but also a painful reminder of our physical separation. The war years were particularly hard. The letters were infrequent, and I worried about him, especially given the Nazi threat which could never be entirely dismissed, even in neutral Switzerland.'

'In a way, it's quite ironic that a man celebrated for his humanity left two of his children behind, abandoned them even, both Lieserl and Tete,' I state, fixing him with a cold stare.

'As I've said, I've never pretended to be perfect, let alone the perfect father. I guess I was just another workaholic parent consumed by his career, letting family life sail by him and it's not something I'm particularly proud of,' he replies, remorsefully.

'Newton's Third Law at work again,' I muse out aloud, waiting for his reaction.

He cocks his head and squints at me, his curiosity piqued. 'Your meaning being?'

'Well, the Third Law, that for every action, there is an equal and opposite reaction, doesn't just apply to physical forces.

It also applies to the metaphysical, meaning everything we experience and *do* in life also has an equal and opposite reaction, or an opposing consequence as I like to term it. For example, for every benefit received throughout life, there will always be an equal and opposite detriment, even though that detriment is often not immediately obvious – nothing is for free right!?'

Einstein frowns, his eyebrows drawn together, obviously not quite following me. 'Okay, take yourself for example: you strived *and* succeeded to unlock some of the deepest mysteries of science at great benefit to yourself in terms of intellectual and professional fulfilment, but...the detriment – or opposite reaction – was equally as great in terms of sacrificing the joys and fulfilment of fatherhood, as you just told me. Examples abound everywhere, from the sublime to the ridiculous – if we just we care to look. A society that benefits from an abundance of cheap fossil fuel pays in the next generation with disastrous climate change impacts: forest fires and floods and the like. The Swiss turophile who enjoys Gruyère and Emmental today, pays years later with arteriosclerosis. The punter who wins big on the lottery then spends a lifetime worrying about protecting her riches – and so on. Newtown was simply reflecting a universal truism, but only through the narrow lens of physical forces.'

'Interesting, hmm,' he muses, raising his shaggy eyebrows. 'But probably fallacious!' he quickly adds. 'For instance, I've enjoyed many a picnic on a warm summer's day – I am indeed a turophile,' He smiles. 'But I don't recall any so-called "negative consequences." My arteries are – *were* – still in good shape.'

I nod in return, having expected this response. 'Maybe you didn't live long enough for that imperceptible melanoma on the back of your neck – caused by the sun's UV rays on those hot summer days – to turn malignant.' I smile as Einstein involuntarily brushes the back of his neck. 'Or maybe you and your picnicking companions spread your blankets on the last scenic spot on one of those packed Sundays on the shores of Lake Zurich, forcing the party behind you to spend their afternoon eating their Landjäger and Appenzeller by the tram tracks, depriving them of the pleasures of the lakeside.'

'I see' he remarks, a sparkle returning to his eyes. 'And does this equal and opposite force exert itself when the initiating event, or action, is a *detriment* and not a benefit?'

Einstein wets his fingers with his tongue and tries to smooth down his unruly moustache, something I note is an unconscious habit of his.

'Yes, of course, it's a bidirectional paradigm, causing a reaction in either direction relative to the initiating event. For example, if I swerve to avoid a cat in the street and accidentally knock a boy off his bike and kill him – rue the thought – that is clearly a detrimental event: the poor boy is dead. However, if as a result of this tragedy, the local legislature is moved to pass a law requiring speed bumps to be placed in all residential streets, then other young lives are likely to be saved in the future, hence a beneficial reaction occurs. The departing point, however, with Newtonian physics is both "time" and "space." The equal and opposite reaction takes place in most cases in *time (t) plus one* and *space (s) plus one,* that is to say, at a future point in both time and space, whereas with physical forces, the reaction happens immediately and adjacent to the initiating action, that is in *t plus zero 0* and *s plus zero.*'

'Hmm, I see and why is that?'

Einstein appears genuinely curious about my theory, one that I've developed over the years based on my own experiments and observations and one that neatly aligns to Newtonian physics. In my mind, Einstein's curiosity in my theory only serves to highlight his rare intellect, especially since my contemporaries, including even my own mother, lazily dismiss this theory as "kooky."

'Because the transmission medium between action and reaction follows a "random walk" trajectory, that is to say, with only a faintly discernible path across time and space. The connection between the action and reaction is often not obvious to most eyes, unlike with physical forces,' I reply.

Einstein claps his hands together and bursts into a delighted laugh, realization suddenly dawning on him. "Bravo, bravo! You might be onto something here, my boy! I'll keep my eyes open next time I'm cutting the cheese!" I smile, deeply satisfied that I've connected on the intellectual level to a fellow pioneering scientist!

Glancing at the clock, I realise it's time to shift the conversation onto a totally different trajectory: women, or rather, womanizing!

'Putting the cheese aside for now, it's fair to say you were quite the "lady's man," is it not?' I state, deliberately taking him by surprise.

Einstein, caught off guard, pushes his wild hair back from his reddening face. 'I'd hardly say that,' he replies sheepishly with a nervous little smile.

'As soon as you entered the Swiss Federal Polytechnic, you attracted the attention of the few female students there, did you not? Your charisma and charm, combined with your aura as a scientific prodigy in the making, caused you to break a few hearts when you left two years later to finish your studies at the Argovian cantonal school.'

He looks at me, still embarrassed, shifting in his chair. 'There were three great loves in your life were there not? Marie, Mileva and Elsa.'

'Actually, two,' he replies in a matter-of-fact way, recovering his balance.

'Two?' I repeat, a little surprised, looking at my notes again.

'Yes.' He leans forward slightly. 'If truth be told my love life was more Shakespearean tragicomedy than Erol Flynn movie. While Mileva was my first wife, Marie was my first love. We met while I was lodging at her father's house, and we became romantically involved, an "affaires de coeur" you might say, right under his nose. It was all furtive snatched moments of passion behind locked doors, with ears wide open for footsteps coming down the corridor. Comical really.' He laughs.

'The unrequited love and tragic farce of Romeo and Juliet, or the racial bigotry and familial disapproval of Othello and Desdemona?' I ask, half jesting.

'Both. In fact, didn't both *end less than well*?' He smiles, clearly enjoying his own Shakespearean allusion, to which I smile appreciatively. 'The situation became untenable under Professor Winteler's roof, and I moved out soon after I enrolled at the Zurich Polytechnic in 1896. I suspect he and Frau Winteler knew what was going on and the good Professor pulled some strings to get Marie a teaching post in Olsberg, far away from the raffish "prodigy in the making." I soon after met Mileva at the Polytechnic. It wasn't what you'd call love at first sight, I wasn't physically attracted to her as such, but she was intellectually appealing and her determination to succeed in a field dominated by men was inspiring. We were friends at first, but that developed into something more over many late nights, shoulder to shoulder, working together on the embryonic "Annus Mirabilis" papers.

'We eventually got married in 1904, partly because we felt it was the right thing – the conventional thing – to do and I guess, to avoid the risk of having another child out of wedlock, you know, after the, erm, *situation* with Lieserl a few years earlier. But if truth be told, I never let go of Marie, emotionally I mean, and a flame burned for her inside me. As faithless as it sounds, I would lie awake at night next to Mileva after we got married, feeling like a fraud, that I was in the wrong bed, dwelling on the life Marie and I could never live together, wishing it was her next to me. It wasn't fair on Mileva of course; she deserved better than that, much better and we divorced some years later, which I can only blame myself for.' He sighs and looks away from me.

'And what of Elsa? Didn't the flame pass from Marie to her?'

'I'd known Elsa since childhood in Germany; we were cousins in fact, and we'd always been deeply fond of each other. That fondness blossomed into...well... romance when I moved to Berlin with Mileva and the boys in 1914. We became intimately involved, almost immediately. She gave me a sense of wholeness, of being wonderfully alive – something I hadn't felt since Marie, I guess,' he says wistfully. 'I knew she was the woman I wanted to be with for the rest of my life. Our relationship was barely a hidden secret, something that was almost flaunted – unintentionally of course – in front of Mileva and she soon moved back to Zurich with the children, for which I could hardly blame her. We divorced some five years later, and I married Elsa with almost indecent haste, according to some wagging tongues, as soon as the divorce papers were finalised.'

'And were there any other special women in your life after you married Elsa? Fidelity not being your strongest suit and all?' I ask insinuatingly, probing to see if anything else will fall out of the tree.

He responds with a louche smile, 'Well, I guess science is... hmm... kind of sexy. After all, there's a lot of creative energy flying around that needs to find an outlet somewhere.' He winks at me playfully. Check. Nice response Albert, I think to myself.

'So, you and Elsa both emigrated to the United States in 1933, which in hindsight proved to be a masterly move, given the horrors of the holocaust that came later,' I state soberly.

'Hmm, you didn't need to be a genius to see what was coming,' he states with equal sobriety. 'If you understood the history of the Jewish people in Europe, it wasn't hard to identify Nazism as the latest incarnation of a historic pattern of antisemitism. In some ways, it was another pogrom, albeit writ large, trading on the old blood libel trope, conjuring up stereotypes of the hooked nose money lender – the Merchant of Venice – the crucifiers of Jesus and so on. It was a simple but depressingly effective formula: whipping up a climate of hatred, scapegoating "the other" as the cause of all society's ills in order to raise yet another ambitious demagogue to power. And we still fall for it don't we,' he adds darkly.

'This time though, there was something deeply rooted, an existential evil whose tendrils crept into every crevice of society, strangling good will and decency, poisoning the very well of reason and sanity. And of course, supercharged by a sophisticated propaganda machine that could carry the message into every street, home, and workplace, the Nazis being masters of media manipulation.' Einstein pauses, ruffling his mane, a contemplative look on his face. 'Sigmund – Freud, I mean – and I discussed the rising tide of Nazism many times together. He took a particular interest – you know both he and Hitler shared Austrian and Jewish backgrounds? He observed significant psychopathological traits in Hitler's speeches and writings in the early Thirties and feared for the worst if his mental illness – as he defined it – went untreated, or at least if his worst instincts weren't checked by those around him – sycophants and self-servers all of them anyway,' he adds with disgust.

'In fact, Freud was fascinated by Hitler from a clinician's point of view and half-joked how he'd love to get him on the couch, for psychoanalysis I mean.' Einstein smiles grimly. 'His enthusiasm was almost childlike when it came to hypothesizing the myriad disorders that Hitler suffered from, everything from Nietzsche's "superman" syndrome to revulsion at his own Jewish blood, and to Freud's own pet oedipal complex. Hitler was a psychologist's A to Z according to good old Sigmund!' Einstein shakes his shaggy head.

'And Freud also suggested there's a constant struggle within each of us, between good and evil; light and dark; peace and violence,' I add, drawing on my own recent conversation with Freud. 'A struggle intrinsic to the very essence of being human. And on top of that he argued leaders, rulers – be it dictator, demagogue, whoever – can either nurture and promote the collective good in humanity or manipulate our darker sides towards hatred and violence for their own selfish gains, normally power and money.

'He also believed that Hitler understood this perennial struggle in man's soul and skilfully exploited it to his own ends – as do so many politicians and rulers today, as I'm sure you'd agree.'

'Hmm, indeed and unfortunately it didn't end with Hitler,

did it? Politicians and would-be demagogues are still whipping up hatred of immigrants, Muslims – whomever the *outsider du jour* is – to serve their own political interests on the ladder to power. But anyhow,' Einstein says, straightening his back and leaning forward, 'all friend-Freud's theorizing became only too real for me in the summer of 1933, when the Nazis declared me a public enemy of the Reich, branding me an insidious influence on German culture and morality and a traitor to the Fatherland.

'They even placed me on their most wanted list, or as they charmingly referred to it, the "not yet hanged list," with a bounty of half a million dollars, in today's money, on my head. Imagine my shock and horror upon discovering they had set such a meagre price for me, Alfred Einstein!' He chuckles at his self-deprecating gallows humour, making light of the matter, whether genuinely or for show, it's hard to tell. 'However,' he continues in the same vein, 'I understand that none other than Herr Goebbels himself added me to the list, so I couldn't have been entirely insignificant, could I?"

'Levity aside, being named a wanted man with a bounty on your head must have been rather, erm, disconcerting. I mean your own country of birth turning against you so capriciously, for no other reason than your religion.'

'Of course, of course, it was a blow, no doubt about it, even though it was half-expected. But one must move on, right? No point feeling sorry for oneself,' he states cheerily. 'And besides, I was one of the lucky ones. I managed to get out in time, whereas many didn't.'

'That must have been difficult, I mean leaving behind so many friends, family and colleagues, that ultimately didn't survive the holocaust. Did you have any feelings of guilt, what I guess Freud would today call "survivor's guilt?"

'There's always guilt, or at least regret. But it's a futile emotion; it only adds to the stock of negative force in the universe. The rational scientific approach is to move forward and to continue to try and do good, to exert positive energy,' he declares, pushing his shoulders back and lifting his chin.

'Was your life ever actually in danger? I mean, did the Nazis ever try to make good on their desire to, err, hang you?'

'There were several attempts on my life, but nothing came of them. They were all rather, how should I say, *amateurish*, actually,' he chuckles dismissively.

'What happened, exactly?' I ask, pressing the point.

'Well, if you must know," he responds, blushing slightly, 'the Nazis raided my cottage in northern Germany, hoping to catch me napping, so to speak. However, I was in Belgium at the time – sloppy, very sloppy intelligence on their part." He shakes his head, almost disappointed at their lack of professionalism. 'Their second attempt to nab me was much better. They tried to grab me off a street in Antwerp and bundle me into the back of a car, but they fumbled the operation and fled once a group of passersby got involved. After that, I didn't trust my luck to hold out for a third time, so I took the prudent step of leaving the Continent for England. Even on the boat from Oostende, I sensed I was being watched and maybe in some danger, although I couldn't be certain. I didn't relax until I disembarked in Dover.'

'Did you feel physically safe once the Channel was between you and the Nazis?'

'Not entirely,' he replies, fiddling with his moustache. 'You've got to remember that fascism had reared its ugly head even in liberal England. There was, of course, Oswald Mosley and his Brown Shirts and their linkages with the National Socialist party in Germany. So, there was still some danger. In fact, British Intelligence had their own concerns for my safety, and they insisted – despite my protests – of posting armed guards to watch over the cottage I stayed in outside London – somewhere in Kent if I recall. But nothing untoward occurred during my stay there, at least as far as I'm aware.'

'I believe you met Churchill while you were in England.'

'Yes, I did.'

'You must have made quite an impression on him.'

'Really? Why?' He raises his bushy eyebrows.

'In the Cabinet papers that were declassified in the Fifties, he states that, and I quote: "I can be bold enough to state to you that Professor Einstein will prove to be a valuable ally in the conflicts that we will soon face, and he must be supported by all means possible." He then goes on to claim that: "Einstein may be as important to the war effort as the North Atlantic convoys and Fighter Command will prove to be. Mark my words gentlemen!" Those are quite extraordinary statements, are they not? What earned you such high praise?'

'Well, that was very kind of Mr. Churchill,' he blushes again. 'And it's true to say we did build a rapport and a certain mutual, how shall I say, *understanding*. Although some of that is still classified to this day,' he hastily adds. 'The Prime Minister does, however, overstate my contribution, which really was no more than the efforts of someone concerned about the fate of fellow Jewish scientists still in Germany. I hardly think my actions can compare to Spitfires doggedly defending the Kent and Sussex coast from fleets of marauding Messerschmitts.'

'So, what exactly *were your* contributions to the war effort?' I probe.

'I was very concerned about the fate of Jewish scientists, as I said and lobbied hard to find them posts in overseas institutions in order to encourage them to leave Germany. Mr. Churchill became immediately interested in this work when I mentioned it to him. In fact, I was surprised how much it resonated with him; so much so that he assigned several Cabinet members to work with me and even sent his friend, the physicist Frederick Lindemann, to Germany to convince Jewish scientists to come over to Britain. What became known to me some time later – after I had signed the Official Secrets Act – was that the British were very interested in, or should I say concerned with, German research into liquid propelled rocket engines.

'The likes of Heinkel and Hellmuth Walter had begun work on a rocket powered aircraft that, in theory at least, could fly faster and out manoeuvre any conventional fighter plane by far. This caused serious angst amongst the RAF top brass, for obvious reasons, making them determined to either get ahead of the Germans or somehow hamper the German program. British Intelligence had a list of scientists that were key to the German's efforts, of whom many were Jewish. Mr. Churchill's idea was to bring these scientists over to England to disrupt the German program while simultaneously accelerating Britain's.'

'And so, you played a pivotal role in persuading these scientists to come to Britain?'

'Well, I played *a* role. I knew some of them personally and others I could reach out to through my contacts. So yes, I worked closely with the British to negotiate to bring them over. At first our efforts resulted in only a frustrating trickle but over time we had so many scientists coming across the Channel that Mr. Churchill joked he'd have to build several new universities to accommodate them all.' Einstein chuckles. 'As it turned out, this exodus of talent set Messerschmitt's rocket plane – the "Komet" – back several crucial years, rendering it virtually ineffective as a super weapon by the time it became operational in 1944.'

'This was one of the unsung victories of the war effort though, was it not? Declassified cabinet papers,' which I have in my hand and make a show of displaying to him, 'reveal that RAF Bomber Command feared the Komet could have eviscerated British and American bombing sorties over Europe, severely limiting the allies' ability to strike at the German heartland. Churchill even posited that the Komet could have extended VE day by another eighteen months. Seen in this light your efforts are more than simply *playing a role,* are they not?!'

'Again, I'm sure this must be an exaggeration,' he smiles modestly.

'There was of course another German super weapon that could have changed the course of the war, or at least extended it, if it hadn't also been starved of Jewish scientific oxygen, wasn't there?'

'What are you referring to?' he asks, furrowing his brow.

'The flying bomb. The V2. The German rocket program – Wernher von Braun's "Terror from the Skies." Hitler and von Braun planned to mass produce a lighter, far more accurate variant of the V2, code named the "Mephistopheles," with the ability to strike allied naval facilities on the English coast, facilities that were essential to the D-Day landings. In addition, if the invasion forces made it onto the Normandy beaches, the Mephistopheles would have been waiting for them, wreaking havoc on the landing zones, turning the beaches into a firestorm that could have prevented an allied breakout from the beach heads. But fortunately, the Mephistopheles program was thwarted by an inability to achieve scientific breakthroughs on two crucial fronts, both that Jewish emigres to Britain were on course to solve.'

'A lot of that remains classified, even after all this time,' he states, with a serious look. 'But yes, your outline is broadly correct. Von Braun was a brilliant rocket scientist, the foremost engineering mind of his time in my opinion, but like all great scientists he had his Achilles heel, or I should say his work did.'

'And that was?'

'Weight to thrust ratios and fin tails,' Einstein states enigmatically, while smoothing his moustache.

I raise my eyebrows.

'Let me explain then,' he sighs gently. 'The keys to an efficient rocket strike capability are *weight* and *accuracy*. The lighter the fuselage and payload the further the rocket will fly with a given amount of fuel. Also, the lighter the material the rocket is fabricated from, the more rockets you can produce from a finite amount of resources. Both the V1 and V2 were heavy, and von Braun needed a breakthrough in lightweight composite materials in order to achieve his "Mephistopheles moment" and a breakthrough that eluded him with the exodus to England of the best minds in composite science. It was a similar story with accuracy.

'Accuracy is determined largely by gyroscopes and fin tails, particularly in the descent stage of the trajectory. To improve accuracy to the point whereby you could land a Mephistopheles on a troop ship moored to a floating quay in Portsmouth, you needed extremely fine precision milling of guidance and stabilizing fins, to tolerance levels that von Braun's machine tools couldn't achieve. So, the Mephistopheles remained an aspiration on paper, and the Germans had to fall back on the blunt instrument that was the V2.'

'Very good, very good. But nonetheless there's a large dose of irony in all this isn't there?' I state accusingly.

'What do you mean?' Einstein replies hesitantly, unsure of my meaning.

'Okay. So, on one hand you were instrumental in the still-birth of the Mephistopheles, a weapons program that could have severely dented the allied war effort, while on the other hand, you helped father an even more deadly weapons program, one that would prove decisive for the allies but deadly for the Axis powers and maybe mankind one day!'

'You're talking about the Manhattan Project I presume,' he states cautiously, averting my scrutiny.

'Yes, the atomic bomb, the weapon that finally ended the war in the Pacific.'

'The Allies didn't take seriously the German's "Uranprojekt" – their atomic bomb program – despite the insistent warnings of émigré scientists such as Wigner and Szilárd,' he responds frowning. 'Roosevelt was too preoccupied with other matters and his general staff dismissed the concept as, well, too far-fetched...'

'However,' I interrupt, jutting my chin out, staring at him intently, 'you feared what an atomic armed Germany could do with such a monstrous weapon and added your voice to the alarm call. Your letter you wrote, along with Szilárd, to Roosevelt and your subsequent visit to the Oval Office nudged – or should I say *compelled* – the President into taking the threat seriously. Thus, the genesis of the Manhattan Project, and I quote Roosevelt: "if a man of Mr. Einstein's pre-eminence, a scientific colossus of our age and a man who has more experience than anyone in this Office of combatting the Nazis, believes this to be so, then I'm bound to defer to him and give all weight and credibility to this threat and the need for the United States to commence on our own great endeavour to develop an atomic bomb, with all haste." However, it strikes me as ironic, to put it mildly, that one of the era's most preeminent humanists and indeed pacifists would light the fuse on a weapons program that ultimately led to the deaths of quarter of a million civilians in Japan and cast the post War World Era under the pall of atomic annihilation for decades to come!'

Einstein looks away, avoiding my stare and sighs heavily, his shoulders dropping. 'Sometimes survival in the present outweighs any considerations of the future,' states quietly.

'What do you mean by that?'

'Without preserving the present, there may be no future, or at least not a future that is worth contemplating. The imperative was to beat the Nazis in a race to the atomic bomb, period. In my opinion, they would have had no compunction in using such a weapon – especially if their backs were against the wall – with all the untold death and destruction that would have entailed in Europe,' he says, crossing his arms in a gesture that seems both defiant and apologetic at the same time.

'Yes, but the Nazis were never *really* close to developing anything resembling a functioning atomic bomb, were they?! Their scientific base was denuded by your own program of Jewish emigration, and they had more pressing needs to deploy their dwindling scientific resources to. In fact, their atomic bomb program was scuttled as early as autumn 1942!' I assert.

'True, true, all very true, but that's with the benefit of hindsight of course. At the time, we had little way of knowing if they would eventually be successful or not. And we couldn't take any risks, could we? Surely not? Germany with an atomic bomb? That was both simply unimaginable and unacceptable! It was the ultimate apocalyptic scenario and had to be stopped by all means possible, regardless of both unknown and unintended future consequences,' he states resolutely.

'Nevertheless, you helped place humanity under the constant threat of extinction, right up until the end of the cold war. Surely you must have some regrets?' I challenge him, my voice rising.

'As I mentioned before, regrets serve no purpose. What I did at the time was driven by scientific reasoning *and* the imperative to save humanity, as I saw it then. That there were negative and unintended consequences – of equal and opposite effect – is something that weighed heavily, very heavily upon me until the day I died. I suppose, in some ways, I entered into a Faustian compact, but unlike Dr. Faustus, I didn't know the Devil's price at the time.' He slumps in his chair and looks down at the ground.

'The Third Law at work writ large, metaphysically speaking,' I suggest.

Einstein looks up and gazes at me dolefully. So, that's settled, I think to myself. It's time to move on from Nazis and weapons of mass destruction and instead get back to basic science and, in particular, apples and stones.

'Most of your great work was produced well before the War, in fact even before the First World War... and some might say you peaked a bit too early – though I wouldn't be so unkind,' I add with a faint smile. 'So, I'm curious, how influential were earlier scientific pioneers in informing your own work, like Newton, for example? Or perhaps I should ask, how important was it for you to challenge the work of others – again, thinking of Newton here – in order to develop your own theories?'

I tap my finger purposefully on the hardback cover of the book resting on my lap: "The Theory of General Relativity" by Albert Einstein.

'Hmm, "challenge?" I wouldn't say my work rested on challenging anyone,' he replies, crossing his arms and sounding peeved. 'Newton's theory of gravity is totally correct in fact. In his time, all objects could be observed as being acted upon by other objects in proportion to their masses and in inverse proportion to the distances between them. He was able to establish this empirically by observing the stars and planets through the telescopes available to him at the time – which were rather primitive, I must add.

'So therefore, within the limitations of 18th Century optical telemetry, Newton was correct and to the present time remains a colossus of science – I'll put that on the record!' he states confidently, straightening up in his chair. 'After all, moonshots to this very day still rely on Newtonian equations. However,' he pauses, rubbing his chin, 'then along came the "Mercury Conundrum!"'

'The *Mercury Conundrum*?' I repeat.

'Yes. Newtonian mechanics couldn't predict the supposed' – he makes air quotes with his fingers – 'errant orbit Mercury made around our Sun, teasing scientists for nearly two centuries after Newton. Hence, scientific curiosity urged me to bridge the gap between the limits of Newtonian mechanics and the observed reality of Mercury's orbit. You may know' – he glances suspiciously at my copy of Einstein on Einstein by Gutfreund and Renn on the table beside me – 'I conducted many of my experiments in my mind. The blackboard was far too limiting, and it wasn't until I delved into the deepest depths of my intellect – pushing beyond boundaries I'd never tested before – that I had my own Eureka moment! That is to say, spacetime is a fabric, a physical fabric that warps and bends like any common fabric you and I can touch here on Earth!'

He picks at his crumpled shirt to reinforce the point. 'This had to be the case! It could be the only logical explanation for the so-called "Mercury Conundrum!" The Sun's mass causes a dip in the fabric of space, a curved dip, that causes Mercury to chart an irregular rotation around the Sun.' His eyes light up and a wide smile forms on his face.

'And so, your theory of general relativity *and* the ultimate debt it pays to an apple falling to the ground – or maybe onto Sir Isaac's head,' I state. I clear my throat and take a sip of water, 'However, there remains a glaring gap in your own work that has taken several generations of scientific development to resolve, is there not?' I lean forward purposefully, holding up his seminal work to his face. 'The luminescence of your General Theory fades at the centre, or the *singularity*, of a black hole, much like Newton's law failed to illuminate the Mercury Conundrum. You in fact – may I say, rather *conveniently* – state that the laws of physics simply disintegrate and no longer apply at the singularity. But curiously, you didn't offer any alternative theories, not even a hint of one.'

I have given some considerable thought to this glaring omission in his research, having discussed it with other learned men and women and come to the conclusion that Einstein had either reached the outer limits of his own intellect, or had grown old and tired and fallen back to the earthier comforts of his violin and jigsaw puzzles – as well as of course his lifelong passion for the opposite sex.

'However, scientists have now developed a new horizon in physics, beyond the General Theory, known as "Loop Quantum Gravity" theory, that demonstrates that the singularity does not even exist and instead there is a hole that drops you out into another branch of spacetime altogether!'

'Yes, so I've heard, even up here – or is it down here? – and in fact I'm very supportive. Of course, I am. Any research that pushes the boundaries of our understanding and challenges long held assumptions is only to be lauded,' he states rather grandly, wafting his hands around. 'And if truth be told,' he now lowers his voice to a conspiratorial hush and looks furtively around the room, beckoning me closer, 'I was stretching my theories to the point of breaking when it came to formulating the singularity. And in some ways, it was a naughty, maybe even cheap, convenience to state that the laws of physics no longer applied at that point.'

A raffish smile spreads across his face and a light twinkles in his eyes. I laugh out loud. I knew it!

'Okay, so we acknowledge the debt you owe Newton and the debt modern science owes you,' I say, leaning back in my chair, relaxed. 'But I wonder if many people are aware of the gratitude your work owes to that smooth-faced, rough-edged Pharaonic stone resting in the British Museum?'

I refer, of course, to the Rosetta Stone – a piece of Egyptology that baffled scientists with its ancient hieroglyphs and parallel Demotic and Greek texts, defying translation for millennia. Einstein raises his eyebrows, indicating he's missing my point, which I admit is somewhat obtuse.

'Let me explain then,' I smile, perhaps a bit too smugly. 'The system developed by the English scientist Thomas Young to decipher the Rosetta Stone involved a complex series of translational experiments. He matched the known Demotic text with the unknown hieroglyphs inscribed beneath them, eventually leading to a full understanding of the hieroglyphic language of the ancient Egyptians and all we now know about them! As it turns out, and as you know, Young then went on to challenge Newtonian physics – a blasphemy in his day, for which he was drummed out of the Royal Society – by developing his own theory that light is a *wave*, not a set of *particles* as proposed by Sir Isaac.'

'Yes, yes,' Einstein interjects with an uncharacteristic hint of impatience, his usually mild German accent now sounding more pronounced.

'Bear with me, Professor. Recently discovered papers of Young's, bequeathed to Edinburgh University, reveal a fascinating entry in one of his journals. He wrote that his frustration at being unable to prove his hunch that light is a wave was only overcome by revisiting, as a last resort, his work on deciphering the Rosetta Stone. It turns out he adapted the same cognitive experimental processes he had used so successfully before, leading to his Eureka moment. This finally allowed him to develop the theoretical underpinnings for his wave theory, debunking Sir Isaac's particle theory of light at the same time. And of course, your own discovery of the wave-particle duality of light in the 1900s was only made possible by Young's foundational breakthrough a century earlier. So, now you see the connection between your work and the Rosetta Stone!?' I exclaim with satisfaction.

"Hmm, I see. Indeed, an interesting interplay – a random walk of actions and reactions spread across space and time, as no doubt you would tell me,' he states, smiling knowingly at me.

'So, if we leave history behind for a moment and look towards the future, to the next horizon in science, what are some of the major breakthroughs we can expect? Who is the next Einstein or Newton out there?'

Einstein fidgets in response to this question and laughs nervously. 'I don't have a crystal ball.'

'No, but I'm sure you do have a view. Or are at least able to speculate,' I reply, prodding him.

Einstein smooths his moustache, contemplating his response. 'Well, if I had to speculate, there are several areas that I believe will fundamentally change both theoretical and practical physics. You see, one of my enduring regrets and deep frustrations to this day is that I couldn't form a unified theory of physics to bring together all the fundamental forces and elementary particles in the universe into a single framework. Even now, I can't lift the heavy lid that keeps the answer hidden from me. It's close, I think, tantalizingly close, but just always beyond my grasp,' he sighs.

'However, there is hope, so I believe. A major impediment for experimental tests of such unified theories is the sheer quantity of energy needed – simply enormous and indeed wasteful amounts are required. But, with the advent of practical and commercially available nuclear fusion by the middle of this century we will finally have the energy source needed to conduct such large-scale experiments and relatively inexpensively,' he states optimistically, his face brightening up.

'So, fusion power by the 2050's?!' I exclaim, surprised.

'Yes, I'm confident of it,' he states emphatically.

'Well, that is excellent, I must say,' I'm excited at the prospect of limitless safe energy so soon. 'And what else do you see over the horizon?'

'Teleportation!' he responds like a shot, laughing, leaving me unsure if he's being serious or not.

'Teleportation? As in "Beam me up Scottie?" That seems a bit far-fetched doesn't it? Although having said that, I'd happily swap a long-haul flight for the Starship Enterprise's teletransportation room, any day.'

'Hm, well, to be fair, you don't need a crystal ball to see that one coming. Scientists have already teleported electrons between two entangled particles in the laboratory and it will only be a matter of time before they can do it with whole physical objects, such as you, or...an apple and a stone,' he chuckles.

'And dare I ask how long before we see that?'

'Well, I wouldn't give up on your Air Miles just yet. Measuring the quantum state of the billions of atoms that make up the human body is a universe away from measuring the quantum state of a Qubit – but is however a necessary condition to teleporting a human from one point in space to another. Nonetheless, measure it we will!' He beams enthusiastically.

I frown for a moment, puzzled. 'But hang on! Didn't you dismiss quantum entanglement in the 1930's as "spooky action at a distance?"' I state, thumbing through my "Einstein on Einstein." 'Are you now saying you were wrong? Or was that another *naughty* convenience?'

'Not wrong, no, just wrong yesterday but right today and quite possibly wrong again tomorrow,' he replies, a broad enigmatic smile spreading across his face. 'Right and wrong exist in a duality and are entirely dependent upon your relative position in time and space. You see, it's simply the knowledge, the understanding, of science that we possess at any given point in time that determines whether we view something as right or wrong. There are no absolutes, only relativities. Remember, the earth used to be flat until it wasn't, and the sun used to orbit the earth until it didn't.'

'I see,' I respond, furrowing my brow.

'But unravelling the properties of and mastering the entanglement of a pair of particles, this will change the way mankind applies physics to the everyday, especially in fields such as computing!' he states, sitting up straight, beaming. 'Quantum entanglement will have the same revolutionary impact on computational calculations in the twenty-first century as Babbage's Difference Engine did in the nineteenth and twentieth centuries,' he continues excitedly, sweeping back his hair.

'Its use in computing – quantum computing – will quite simply cause a tectonic shift in scientific and technological knowledge! What takes today's computers a hundred years to calculate will be resolved in minutes. Everything as we would otherwise have come to know it will change, accelerate exponentially. Now of course, in line with *your* third law of metaphysics, this awesome amount of computational power will no doubt create unintended and alarming consequences, some known and some not.'

'Can you expand on that?' I edge forward in my seat.

'You see, while some consequences remain unpredictable due to random walk theory, others are known with a degree of certainty. For instance, today's information security relies on asymmetric key cryptography, which scrambles and unlocks data – ranging from personal banking information to military secrets – using digital key pairs. Depending on the key length, it can take decades, if ever, for the most powerful computers to decode these keys. However, with the exponential power of quantum computing, these codes can be cracked within minutes. Imagine that – everything we believed to be secret and secure, suddenly exposed to anyone with access to a quantum computer, from bank thieves to foreign spies! And that's just the beginning.

'Consider the god-like power that will emerge when quantum computing is combined with artificial intelligence. Who knows where that will lead us? Miracle cures for cancers on one hand, and unthinkable biological weapons on the other.'

After this burst of enthusiasm, Einstein sits back in his chair. Moments later, he narrows his eyes, contemplating me, while gently brushing his moustache with his fingers. 'There is one more thing, though,' he adds, his eyes locking onto mine. 'One final puzzle that will be unlocked – eventually, one day,' he says, his voice dropping to a solemn tone. 'Man will look upon the face of God, and on that day, man will see the truth – the truth of the beginning and the truth of the end. And then it shall be.' He pauses, hands resting on his lap, his body in repose, a picture of tranquillity.

'What shall be?' I ask, puzzled, caught off guard by his near-messianic look and tone.

'Man will know what God knows, and then man will be God.' Einstein smiles, an almost beatific look on his face.

I open my mouth to ask the obvious question, but before the words can form, I instinctively decide not to say anything. Einstein gently nods at me, rises stiffly, and looks around before shuffling off to the singular door in the room, beyond which is only he knows. I'm left sitting alone as the door closes behind him, contemplating our extraordinary conversation.

So, Einstein – a towering figure of twentieth-century science; a man whose name became synonymous with genius; a man who personally battled the Third Reich; a man who changed the course of the Second World War; a man who communed with luminaries such as Freud; a man who strived for world peace and justice for mankind; and a man who perhaps, ironically, brought the world to the brink of atomic annihilation. But also – maybe – a man who knows far more about the meaning of life, the universe, and everything than he's deigning to tell us.

A CONVERSATION WITH WILLIAM SHAKESPEARE

'Why did you do it?' I ask.

'Do what?' Shakespeare replies testily, scratching his backside.

'Sculpt your Shylock from the same clay as Marlowe's Barabas,' I reply in a matter-of-fact way.

Shakespeare scoffs, puffing out his chest, clearly not able to resist my jibe that he found inspiration in the character created by Kit Marlowe – the "enfant terrible" of the Elizabethan literary scene – and not the other way around.

'Although both plays are anchored in the Mediterranean-sea, "The Jew of Malta" is but a poor reflection of my "Merchant of Venice,"' he replies haughtily.

'But Marlowe wrote "The Jew of Malta" several years before you wrote the "Merchant of Venice", so how could, as you're suggesting, Marlowe plagiarize your character, unless your play *played* with time itself!' I counter.

He glares at me with barely concealed hostility. 'That is so, but Marlowe fashioned his character after mine. That is the be all and end all of the matter!' he declares, raising his voice while folding his arms defensively across his chest.

'But how can that be?' I ask, refusing to let him off the hook so lightly.

Shakespeare harrumphs. 'Well, if you really must know – and you are a persistent fellow, aren't you – Marlowe and I were different sides of the same creative coin. We shared a common currency in the exchange of ideas – ideas most often fermented in a jar of ale, probably many jars, actually, in the riverside taverns of Southwark. Those hostelries of colourful rogues were fertile breeding grounds for the characters and plots that became the stuff of our plays. I recall one fine evening of revelry – at the "Castell On The Hoop," if memory serves – regaling Marlowe and his company – reprobates and hangers-on the lot of them – with tales of my time spent in the canal-crossed duchy of the Doge, *yes*, Venice!

'It was there that I first encountered that much-maligned class of financiers and conjured up a character from the bottom of a gondola that would be the perfect metaphor for avarice and revenge. Marlowe and I clinked – or was it bashed? – jars back and forth all night, frothing at the possibilities of a play built around such a rapacious character. A character that would have the cheap seats on the edges of their impecunious perches, booing and hissing as the unkindest cut of all sought its fleshy collateral, its *pound of flesh*!"'

Shakespeare leans back, hands clasped behind his head, legs stretched out before him, eying me.

'So, you and Marlowe jointly concocted the trope of the medieval moneylender, basically over a *pint*, but he beat you to the punch: he put quill to paper and player to theatre before you?'

Pricked by his vivid imagery, it's not hard to picture the two literary giants revelling and improvising in the lively, smoke-filled haunts of the literati; those dens of iniquity along the south bank of the Thames. But on the other hand, I have to wonder whether Marlowe and Shakespeare could really have been each other's muses – the literary odd couple, so to speak – given the fierce competition of the Elizabethan theatre scene?

'That's the long and short of it,' Shakespeare replies with surly indifference, whether feigned or real, I'm not sure, as he proceeds to pick his teeth and inspect the rewards of his work.

'If that's so, and let's say it is, then why create a character, no, a whole narrative, that vilifies a religion and reinforces prejudices as opposed to challenging those prejudices and seeking to educate and enlighten?' I contest, while at the same thinking I maybe applying a twenty first century view to a sixteenth century paradigm.

'I'll let Barabas be the mouthpiece for Marlowe, but I can tell you' – and he leans forward fixing me with his glassy eyes – 'Shylock mouthed as any man, be that man Christian, Jew, or Mussulman. A man that bleeds like any other; a man that feels pain like any other; a man that loves his children like any other; a man that seeks redress for wrongs like any other. In essence, a man that only seeks to be treated like any other man – because underneath our garb we're all the same blood and bone, sweat and tears, hates and fears, and in the cold embrace of death, nothing but the same earthy food for the insensible worms, who care nothing of our creed. That was the message, the essential meaning, that Shylock gave to my audiences: the universality of man!' he declares with passion, rising tall in his chair, his cheeks flushed red and spittle collecting at the corners of his mouth.

'So, if you intended to cause your audience to feel sympathy, or even empathy, for the plight of the persecuted Jew, as personified by Shylock, why did you make him so furiously intractable, so...unfeeling and inhumane in his singular insistence for enforcing the letter of the law...for taking his *pound of flesh*? Doctor Balthasar gave him ample opportunity, even beseeching him several times, to take the gold instead, and in the noble guise of being merciful...yet Shylock's cruel, vengeful knife was only parried in the end by the cutting legal riposte of that charlatan barrister!' I state, not with a little passion myself, referring to Shakespeare's character Portia, who disguises herself as the fictitious lawyer Doctor Balthasar to defend the debtor Antonio in the case brought against him by Shylock.

Shakespeare wipes his mouth with the back of his lace-trimmed sleeve, now marred by stains and then breaks wind loudly. 'But that is the point, that is exactly the point! Shylock has the right to behave in the same way as do his Christian interlocutors: to be as cold and callous as they; to be as hard and unfeeling as they; to be as devious and dogmatic as they. Why should a Jew – or a Mussulman, come to that – be expected to behave differently, more magnanimously, than a Christian, just because he doesn't recognise Jesus to be the son of God!' Shakespeare declares fervently, waving his hands animatedly and leaning in closer to me, so close that I can smell the stale beer on his breath combined with the sour odour of someone who has been carousing all night, still wearing the same clothes.

'Big night at "The Castell On The Hoop" was it?' I ask, raising my eyebrows, to which he grunts, pulling back from me.

'So, let me ask you this: while laudable, it's nonetheless highly unusual for a sixteenth century Protestant playwright to be a torch bearer for religious tolerance. So, why you?'

Shakespeare harrumphs in response to this question, a dark look forming on his face. He's clearly not impressed.

'Do you not think your message of religious tolerance was a little, erm, out of kilter for your times?' I continue, pushing for a response.

He pauses as if weighing his words before responding: 'As with all good tales, there's more to it than meets the eye, but that's a tale for another time.'

Absolutely, my curiosity is now fully piqued! I lean in, sensing a story here: 'Alright, let's hear it then, this "tale!"' I urge him.

To which he responds, hackles bristling, with a thunderous reply: 'God's blood! Drop the bone, cur!'

I gasp; eyes wide open! I've never been spoken to like that before during a conversation, especially not in Elizabethan English and certainly not by a playwright from the Southbank. I'm unsure whether to be insulted or amused.

Either way, an awkward silence ensues, which is only broken when he suddenly softens, a sheepish grin spreading across his face. 'Forgive my outburst,' he says, leaning forward, clapping me on the shoulder. 'Passions run high in the theatre, you understand.'

Particularly after a big night out on the piss I think to myself, wrinkling my nose. 'No offence taken.'

'Shall we move on then?' he asks very politely, to which I tip my head in agreement.

Clearing my throat, somewhat theatrically, as a reset, I continue: 'You mentioned something else that caught my ear. You said you were in Venice, and that's where you were inspired to create the character of Shylock. But did you mean you were *literally* in Venice, or did you mean you were there *figuratively* speaking, in one of your, uh, moments of literary inspiration in the taverns of Southwark?

'And the reason I ask is because there is no record of you having ever left England. In fact, your life is a blank canvas from 1585 to the summer of 1592 – you might as well have been slumbering in "sweet repose" with Oberon and Titania in fairy land, for all the records we have of you during this time.'

Shakespeare laughs. 'I've strode the Rialto itself, or should I say more accurately, been dangled by my feet from its sides, staring down at a watery death below.'

'So, you did visit Italy?' I ask, unsure if his response is merely theatrical.

'Indeed, I did. No less than three years I spent in that peculiarly wonderful peninsula of palazzos and piazzas,' he replies, beaming at me.

'And what circumstances led you there, may I ask?'

'A short but violent passage across the sea and then a long muddy slog by horse and carriage across France, and there I was,' he replies being deliberately obtuse.

'I see' – being deliberately patient in the face of his obtuseness – 'but why were you there at all? I mean it wasn't a common holiday destination for Elizabethan Englishmen was it.'

'Why does one need a purpose to be in Italy? To be in Italy *is the* purpose. To be in Italy, or not to be in Italy? That is the question all aspiring poets and artists must ask themselves. As marble is to the sculptor, is Italy to the playwright: the richest palette of life, love, lust, comedy, tragedy, pathos, intrigue, cruelty, and greed. Go to Italy with a blank canvas and come back with a Renaissance masterpiece, in all its richness of colourful drama. To produce wonderful art, you must immerse yourself wonderfully in art!' Shakespeare exclaims with a theatrical flourish, having visibly perked up from his earlier hungover state.

However, I'm none the wiser whether this is all an act, or he's being fulsome with the facts, and he evidently senses my hesitation.

'The Bassanos of Bishopsgate' – he continues, by way of an explanation – 'Italian Jewish troubadours whose acquaintance I made while living in London, and with whom I happily agreed to journey to Italy as a traveling player in their company – seeking fame, fortune, and grist for my poetic mill – and a warmer bed than the cold comfort offered by the ladies of London,' he adds with a raffish wink.

'So, Rome, Verona, Venice, Milan, Padua, I presume?' musing out aloud, still not entirely sure of what is fact and what is fiction.

'Yes of course, all of those, and you'll probably still find my signature in some dusty tome as a guest at the venerable English College in Rome, if you look hard enough,' he states confidently.

'So, we can assume on your travels throughout Italy you took in the scenes, sets, and characters that later became the material for your plays?' I ask.

'Yes, *we* can assume. What richer source material is there than life itself?!' he confirms.

'Well, can you fill in the missing pages of your personal history for us then? I'm sure the world would love to hear about it.'

'You can read my plays, it's all in there.' he laughs playfully. 'But no, of course I'd be happy to share some of the principal scenes with you, if you're *really* interested. So, where do I start?' he asks rhetorically, tapping his top lip with his finger, as if deep in thought. 'Well, I was a soldier, sailor, lover, actor, pauper, and dead man, but never a gentleman I hasten to add, that came later!' he chuckles.

'Once the Bassanos, and I parted ways, I was befriended by a Moorish sailor in Venice, actually more mercenary than sailor, who taught me the disingenuous art of war. But being more disposed to wound the heart with a love poem, than pierce a man with cold heartless steel, I fear I was a poor student of soldiering. My Moorish friend, however, had an abundance of patience, and with him I entered the ranks as a soldier of fortune, in the service of *La Serenissima*,' he exclaims with a flourish.

'A mercenary!' I exclaim surprised. 'Did you actually do any fighting?' I can't quite picture Shakespeare the pugilist in my mind.

'I brandished my sword in the general direction of a few Ottomans and Genoese, albeit from behind the shadows of my large Moorish friend and that seemed enough to earn me the Doge's ducat. However, after a year, or thereabouts, I confirmed what I always knew: that I was more poet than pugilist – though not quite a heartless hind – and so bid a farewell to arms. But I should add, I had occasion to make good use of my new-found sword play later in life, in company with my fellow thespians of the Lord Chamberlain's Men!' He laughs at his self-deprecating humour.

'So, Shakespeare the soldier! That's certainly a turn up for the cards. We think of you in contemporary terms as more lover than fighter.'

'It was not a thing of substance, so don't overplay it. My part was small, backstage stuff really. The tough men of war though, they were something else, like my Moorish friend, full of foul language; festooned in tattoos and scars; brimming in arrogance and pride; lightening quick to the quarrel; seeking fame and fortune and caring only for the moment. Such warlike cloth I was not cut from, save and except I could stand shoulder to shoulder with any of them – even higher – when it came to wielding those deadly weapons of the drinking man: a jar of ale and a bottle of wine!' he exclaims, chuckling again.

For my part, I can't help but conjure up images of the Bard in a dark smoky tavern, inveigling himself with his soldierly companions through his witty repartee and foolish antics: jumping up on rough long tables and kicking off plates and cups to clear a stage to lead his company in rumbustious drinking songs. Songs that no doubt contained lascivious chorus lines featuring poor maidens and the indignities they suffered at the less than honourable hands of his fellow mercenaries. As he says, probably more regimental mascot than regimental champion.

'So, what of love may I ask?'

'After soldiering, which as I said I soon grew tired of, after a few too many close scrapes, I returned to playing and singing and embraced the Bassanos once more. They'd risen in the world from country fair comedies and tavern ticklers to private performances for the lords and ladies of St. Mark's Square, and it was there that I then found myself within the range of the perfumed princes and princesses of *La Serenissima*, the serene Republic. Being an Englishman and one with a colourful tale to tell, I naturally stood out, attracting the attention of the fairer sex. And that's how I met her, no, saw her, first! The loving archer shot an arrow straight through my heart – a truer aim no fellow soldier of mine ever had – and I dropped to the floor smitten by the "coup de foudre," clutching my breast, where my stolen heart once beat!'

Shakespeare theatrically clutches both hands to his chest with a look of feigned anguish on his face. 'Now, of course, a noble lady of the Venetian court was far too high born for the likes of a Stratford lad to win her family's approval, and so, I courted her from the shadows, and once she was mine and I hers, our affairs of love were conducted in disguise and deceit: in the bottom of gondolas; in the back of palazzos; high up in towers, anywhere but in front of the public gaze. So of course, you can imagine where this torrid tale of two socially unmatched love birds led...' he pauses, peering at me with an expectant look on his face.

'To a sword fight, deadly elixirs of the night and so on,' I reply, a little cynically.

He smiles at me indulgently. 'You've been reading too many plays. We were betrayed by her sister, no less, and that lady I'm sure, had a jealous eye on me. Her father, a leading light of the Republic, set his hounds on me and vicious curs they were too! I was bound and beaten and dropped none too gently into the bottom of a barge and spirited away across the lagoons. Meanwhile my love was handed a letter, a forgery, a fake, meant to be from my own unfeeling hand and callous quill, bidding her a curt farewell as I supposedly set out to return to my native land.

'Well, return to my native land I did not! Despite my roughing up and warning never to return upon pain of death, I returned to her but...' – he stares at the floor, his lips trembling as he struggles to form his words, fighting back a welling emotion – 'but it was too late. She was gone. My world ended. Time stopped. Only the memory of her remained. My sweet love turned to bitter ash in my mouth.' He turns his head away from me, rubbing his eyes, struggling to maintain his composure – or so it seems.

After a few moments, I encourage him to go on. 'You can imagine when she read that fabricated text, her heart was torn in half. But you cannot imagine what she did next! For her too time stood still – or so I pictured in my mind's eye – with only a desolate road ahead, without her sweet William to join her on life's long journey. As true heroines do, she tied herself around the waist with dead weights and leapt from her balcony to a watery grave below. But alas! I didn't have the courage to join her – I was only half the lover of my own Romeo – and as true curs do, I whimpered from tavern to tavern, from day to night, heroically drowning my sorrows in the bottom of a jar, not quite valiant enough to slip into the watery tomb beside her. How long I went on like this I can't tell; weeks, maybe months, maybe even more. Time stood still. But in time, the Bassanos found me under a rock and took me back in, despite the stink and wildness that clung to me.'

He presses his fingers to his temples, shaking his head slowly before releasing a long, rueful sigh. 'The milk of human kindness those Bassanos. They held me close to their bosom and nursed me back to health, and eventually, they even coaxed me back onto the boards, if only for a few bit roles. And then it came to me, a sudden revelation, like Jove's lightning striking from the skies on a still summer's night: it was time to return home! An unbearable aching desire came over me to walk down dappled lanes arched in green and bathed in soft sunlight; to peer up at the ageless towering oaks; to stare upon the bucolic countryside of lush meadows merrily cut by happy English hands; to be lulled into blissful reverie by the enchantress songs of the woodlark and thrush; to brighten with delight as the sweet shy Anemones open their delicate purple faces to greet the change of seasons; to scent the heady rush of the rose as she dispenses her rich bouquet to prince and pauper alike; to glimpse the stealthy fox before his orange haze disappears into hedgerow; and to smile at the squirrel – most marvellous of acrobats – as he leaps and flies in his circus of the air.

'The invisible strings that bind every man to their native soil, regardless of how long and far they travel, tugged at my heart and beckoned me back to sweet England. And so, the decision was made!' he exclaims, straightening up, breaking the pastoral trance. 'But, before I could set off for home, there was a small matter of a large debt that needed to be settled. Drinking oneself to death is no cheap thing, unless death cheats the debt! But I cheated death and not the debt' – he frowns – 'leaving me with an impecunious dilemma and hostile creditors, who were not shy of violence, I may add.'

'Did you slip out of town concealed in the bottom of a barge?' I suggest lightly.

'No, not this time. Come what may, it was time to face the day,' he replies grimly. 'I answered the summons to my final accounting, seeking redemption and if that meant death, then so be it! I would be at least with her. Hence, I found myself hanging headfirst from the Rialto, held by the ankles, roughly shaken and threatened with a drowning if my repayment was not forthcoming.' He shudders, a dark look crossing his face. 'Now, of course, a money lender does not discard an impaired asset like a rotten fish head, otherwise he would not be worthy of his chosen profession and should quite rightly expect his peers to drum him out of their guild of thieves, lest he tarnish their reputation as men of serious business. So up I came, hauled back onto the bridge, wondering what injustice would come next.'

'Yet you were penniless, without collateral. You had nothing to your name, except the clothes on your back.'

'Yes, almost, but not quite. I still had my body, my hands in fact, and that's exactly what was demanded in lieu of my debt.'

'Your hands? They wanted your hands? What, as their *pound of flesh*?' I exclaim in alarm.

'Don't fret,' – Shakespeare chuckles, peering down appreciatively at his fingers and thumbs – 'this particular merchant was not *my* Shylock. And besides, what good would a pound of my flesh be to a wily man of business like Joseph, Joseph Usque, hmm? No! It was my sword hand that was the trade. I was to take Joseph's place in a duel designed to settle some quarrel or other. My reputation as a soldier of fortune having preceded me – although, of course, I was more soldier of misfortune, if truth were told!'

'A duel!?'

'Yes, how farcical!' – he laughs – 'even more so when I squared off with my opponent and looked him in the face. The fight was over before it started. Despite having the poorer sword hand, I still had the upper hand. My opponent keeled over violently, convulsing and clutching his sides, the most deafening booms of thunder erupting from his wounded lips. Will Shakespeare, the master swordsman, ha!' he declares with a flourish, his nose pointing coquettishly to the ceiling. 'Well not quite – more like a master comedian! My opponent took one look at me and was seized by the most violent fits of laughter, causing his mighty heart to burst. Poor fellow.'

'You caused your opponent to laugh himself to death?' I ask confused.

'Well, in a manner of speaking. But the correct question should be: "Who was my opponent?"'

'Go on then, pray tell,' I say encouragingly, playing along.

'It was none other than my Moorish friend!'

I'm shocked to hear this, and it must clearly show. 'Yes. Once he clapped eyes on me, the thought of this yapping puppy nipping at his heels in a mismatched contest, this helpless whelp that had cowered behind his mighty frame, hurling insults at Genoese and Ottoman alike, with the courage of one who knows he'll never be called to account in the fight, was too much for him. It ignited such a hilarious outburst that his innards rented themselves asunder. My poor dear Moor.' He sighs wistfully, wiping his brow. 'But at least he died laughing and in the company of a brother soldier, rather than going lonely and fearful into the night. Oh, happy warrior, Oh happy death.'

'That's terrible! Truly terrible,' I exclaim, lamenting this cruel twist of fate: he whom the Moor befriended and protected so faithfully becoming the unwitting instrument of his own death. 'The gods' truly are pitiless,' I protest.

'Yes, it was tragic, awful. Losing both a lover and a brother in one season was more than one should have to bear,' he says with deep melancholy, shaking his head.

'If nothing else, at least your ledger was now balanced with the money lender, and you had your life back,' I offer sympathetically.

'Yes, I had my freedom and my future, and I could now bid farewell to the watery republic and all her dramas, including *her*.' He sighs again. 'Well, my part was played out, and it was time to dance the jig and take a final bow. I set off for England and before you ask; it was another uneventful journey through France. But I had much time to reflect, as I was bounced and shaken along the rutted road home.

'Italy had given me all the palettes of life, all the casts and characters to populate my future plays – my Italian canvas no less. "The Two Gentlemen of Verona," "Romeo and Juliet," "The Taming of the Shrew," and of course "The Merchant of Venice" and "Othello" – as well as nine other plays – all took shape before I reached Dover. All being expressions of my Italian experiences; retellings of all those scenes I saw and indeed many that I lived through as the principal character – my art imitating my life, you could say,' he adds with a flush of pride.

It's now all too easy for me to see where the inspiration for the Bard's trademark farcical mix ups, unrequited love, tragic deaths, and otherwise, impossible high drama all came from, at least for his works with an Italian accent. But there is one thing that puzzles me, though:

'Did you spend time in Rome, while you were in Italy?'

'Rome?' he responds with a baffled look.

'Yes, Rome. The reason I ask is because your "Roman plays" – "Julius Caesar," "Antony and Cleopatra," "Coriolanus," and "Titus Andronicus" – seem to show, to me at least, a strong affinity for that eternal city and its storied past.'

'Haha, no' – he chuckles – 'while I clambered over the old stones of the Forum and gazed up at the crumbling Colosseum, marvelling at the ancients, my inspiration came from somewhere far more prosaic and closer to home: a grammar school in Stratford no less. They were strong on the classics, you know,' he replies, slapping his thigh. 'That and my friend Thomas North's translation of Plutarch, of course. In fact, those four plays, well three of them anyway, were some of the easiest to write, almost plagiarism you might say!' He grins at me mischievously.

'Plagiarism?' I raise my eyebrows in surprise

He smiles at my obvious concern for literary integrity. 'Well, not exactly but my point being that the facts speak for themselves, the historical facts that is. The plots and characters leap out from the pages of history, bringing their own drama to the stage, with little need for the playwright's artistic embellishment. But I did have fun wagging the characters' tongues with my own fair words,' he adds enthusiastically. 'Think of Mark Antony's eulogy in "Julius Caesar." Think how I make his speech the stick that stirs the passions of his fellow citizens, igniting their anger at Caesar's assassins and making them pliant to his will.

'Observe how artfully he damns Brutus and the other "honourable men" with faint praise, slowly setting the trap for them, leading them into its vice-like jaws. Witness how he transforms Caesar's flaws into unassailable Olympian virtues, and how he turns the tide of history with only his artful tongue. Stirring words for both the Forum and the stage, although, I do owe a little credit to Plutarch,' he adds modestly.

'I'm sure Caesar would have been chuffed with your glowing funeral oration – he's very sensitive to his image, you know. However, I can assure you that he was not so chuffed, in fact was downright indignant, that you banished him to the darkest corners when it came to the great love affairs of history.'

'How so? What do you mean?' he asks, a concerned frown crossing his face as he leans into me.

'I had the great man in here for a conversation, in the very seat you're sitting in, and I can tell you he was none too happy, blaming you for writing "Antony and Cleopatra" at the expense of his own love affair with the Queen of the Nile,' I explain, voicing indignation on behalf of the Dictator. 'What happened to *Julius* and Cleopatra? Did he not beat Mark Antony to her bed? Did she not dramatically reveal herself to him in that most theatrical of carpet tricks? Did he not bear her to the throne of Egypt, as she bore him a son to Rome? And did he not scandalize Roman society with his barely hidden love affair right under their haughty noses? So, why not *Julius* and Cleopatra?' I continue.

And as an aside, I make a mental note to invite Cleopatra in for a conversation in the near future – it'll be good to get a woman's perspective on all of this.

Shakespeare furrows his brow, clasping his hand to his jaw in a gesture of concern. He looks at me intently, or rather through me, as if trying to unravel a mystery. After a few moments, he slowly relaxes and unexpectedly offers an apology: 'Tell him I'm sorry, I'm genuinely sorry, I really am! I'm one of Caesar's biggest admirers. I intended no insult, I really didn't. If it's any comfort – and if it is, I'm sure it's only cold comfort – it's me who has been injured by this wrong. I can see that now. What a play that would have been: "Julius and Cleopatra!" he exclaims with a heavy sigh.

'I wouldn't worry *too* much about it. I'm sure he's moved on by now. He's probably even reread your lofty funeral oration to make himself feel better,' I say trying to placate the Bard.

'Well, it's not good enough. It's just not good enough! The noble Caesar shall have his love play,' he exclaims, brightening up with a twinkle in his eye. 'Do you have a spare quill and paper?' Without waiting for a reply, he grabs the pen and notepad beside me and proceeds to furiously scribble away, a look of deep concentration etched on his face. After a few minutes: 'Aha! I have it!' he exclaims with boyish glee, brandishing his script in my face. 'Shall I read it to you?'

And before I can reply, he's up on his feet, clearing his throat for attention and then begins reciting the first verses he's penned – or is it quilled? – in over four hundred years!

'"When Julius met Cleo." A poem by William Shakespeare.

Her eyes burn with ambition and fierce intelligence;
Brilliant coals that shine with translucence,
Her obsidian black her, coils of glowing lava,
Her skin as pure as asses' milk;
To the touch but pure silk,
Her scent like Elysian fields of flowers,
Her royal gait hypnotic, causing heads to sway,
Her smile beguiles and disarms,
Her voice honeyed, tantalizes the air,
Her words are wit and wisdom personified,
Her aura, does all in her presence command,
Julius stands transfixed, no words are there.
He the foremost military mind in the world;
Favourite of Mars,
He that no army can defeat;
Spartacus, Vercingetorix and Pompey crushed in the field,
He who outfoxes his enemies from Alexandria to Alesia,
He who would be Dictator of all Rome.

Cleopatra is struck; he would carry her to the throne.
Two burning ambitions, coil in passion,
Fervent lips pressing, tongues searching,
Corn field stubble, teases soft skin,
Bodies embrace, stumble onto brushed cotton,
Mortal garments are shed and torn,
Hands lock, the lovers combine,
Their bodies rhythmically ebb and flow,
Rapid breathes, rising to a crescendo
A moment of ecstatic glory,
As their bodies; their fates are now intertwined.'

Shakespeare looks at me expectantly, searching my face for a response.

'Good, very good. In fact, I like it a lot,' I reply, letting the poem sink in. 'I think Caesar should be happy, knowing he's now bested Mark Antony on all scores,' I chuckle. 'But of course, you'll need to publish it. Caesar's all about publicity and image, you know.'

'Not too bad, not too bad at all, eh.' He strokes his chin, contemplating his work. 'It lacks a certain meter of course – I didn't have time to write it in iambic pentameter – but all the same, given the time pressure, not *too* bad. I think old Julius should like it,' he states with a satisfied smile.

'I just hope by righting a wrong, we haven't wronged a right,' I add, cautiously.

'What do you mean?' He asks, sounding perplexed at my tautology.

'Well, I don't want Mark Antony in here next week complaining that he's been outshone by Caesar through a late appeal to the Bard.'

Shakespeare laughs: 'Very droll. Very droll!'

'So much for the love lives of Julius Caesar and Mark Antony,' I say, preparing to shift the conversation. 'But what about the love life of William Shakespeare?'

He frowns, suddenly looking less certain of himself. 'You

left Anne Hathaway at home in Stratford with your three children to raise on her own, while you embarked on a grand adventure to Italy. There, you had a passionate affair with a woman who seems to have been the true love of your life. So, what was the deal between you and Anne?' I ask, fixing him with a cold stare.

Shakespeare grimaces, obviously feeling the barb. He slowly shakes his head, a look of contrition appearing on his face. 'I can understand how it appears, but love and life are never as they seem. Anne was a good woman,' he continues wistfully, 'a kind woman, a caring mother to our children. She was also a practical and very capable woman, one who could take care of herself and the family. She had that good sense and pragmatism that's often the hallmark of women who grow up on farms.'

'A good woman? A kind and caring mother? That's not quite the view taken by contemporary scholars, who suggest that Anne was a "femme fatale,"' I challenge him. 'A woman older and more experienced than you, who lured you into a hasty marriage via a pregnancy out of wedlock. Some have even gone as far, dare I say it, as to call her a *shrew*.'

The Bard regards me, without any obvious hostility. 'To set the record straight and put all those scurrilous tongues to rest – and besides who are they to judge, they weren't even there – it was *I* who courted Anne, *I* who chased after her and *not* the other way around,' he states with obvious genuineness. 'In fact, if truth be told, she showed little interest in me, at least initially. I think she even found my attention irksome. And besides, I was a young man with few obvious prospects in life. Not exactly a great catch for a lady to the manor born – her father certainly saw it that way,' he adds wryly.

'So why did you leave her for all those lonely years then?'

'It's a fair question. I was a young man in a hurry if truth be told, rushing into bed and marriage with all the impetuosity of youth. But I was determined not to be trapped in a marriage where the bed and heart grew cold over time, staring at a future of domestic mediocrity upon the Avon. After the birth of the twins, Hamnet and Judith, my restlessness became unbearable. I knew I had to spread my wings, make my mark on the world. I even contemplated slipping out of the house in the dead of night, like a thief, simply leaving a note on the pillow,' he laughs bitterly.

'But thank Harry I didn't. Instead, I confronted the matter head-on with Anne. It was a painful conversation for both of us, as you can imagine, and it had its own bitter twist,' he smiles sardonically, 'she didn't love me either. In some ways, this mutual honesty was cathartic for both of us and ironically helped sow the seeds for a deep bond of affection and admiration that grew between us over the years. So, I left for London, with a blessing of sorts, and the rest is history, as you now know.' Shakespeare sighs, his complexion pale. He offers me a weak smile.

'Did these, erm, domestic difficulties in the early years of your marriage influence your plays in any ways? Literary scholars have speculated that "The Taming of the Shrew," for example, may owe something to your relationship with Anne – as unlikely as that now sounds,' I hasten to add.

'No. "The Shrew" had nothing to do with Anne or our life together,' he states emphatically. 'The play was adapted from ballads and folklore about the domination of wives by their husbands, using foul means rather than fair. In truth, some of these sources were little more than crude medieval pamphlets, instructing men how to bend their wives to their will.'

'So, then does "The Shrew" shine a satirical light on misogyny and domestic violence, maybe seeking to challenge your audiences' attitude to women? Or is it a play in sync with its times, encouraging the treatment of women as mere chattels of their fathers and husbands?' I ask, glancing at my notes scrawled around the margins in my copy of "The Oxford Companion to Shakespeare." 'Personally, I've always felt uneasy at the way the principal character, Petruchio, seeks throughout the play to break his newly wed wife's free spirit,' I add, making my own position clear.

'You can read it either way,' he replies thoughtfully. 'The

play offers scope for different interpretations and moral stances, depending on how the actors choose to perform it – how they emphasize aspects of the dialogue and treat the portrayal of the characters. For example, they can treat Petruchio's wife Kate sympathetically as a once independent intelligent woman reduced to domestic servitude by her cruel husband. Or they can treat her as a loud mouthed, insolent wench who is eventually brought to heel and made a respectful and submissive wife by Petruchio's manly handling of her.'

I note that Shakespeare's neutral tone and impartial analysis – or fence sitting – gives nothing away of his own thinking on the matter.

'But what of the play's *author*, which side of the fence does *he* stand on? Kate's or Petruchio's?' I insist on knowing.

'The play's author was a man of his times, not one to disturb the social order of things, but rather to amplify them,' Shakespeare replies, again with an almost purposeful neutrality.

'So, you stand with Petruchio then?' I seek to confirm.

'The author was a man of exceptional literary talent. A titan of verse. One of Europe's finest. A puppet master who could control both the stage and the audience like few others, but nonetheless, a man of scant respect for women, a man who would not have felt uncomfortable in Petruchio's very own company,' he states drily.

Is Shakespeare really saying and with no shame, that he is a misogynist? I ask myself. I really hope I've misunderstood him. 'So, you do stand with Petruchio!'

'As I said to you, the author stands with Petruchio. However, *I* do not. *I* choose to stand with Kate,' he states, seemingly contradicting himself and confusing me at the same time.

'But is that not a blatant contradiction? How can you stand with *both* Petruchio and Kate?' I exclaim, starting to feel a little frustrated with this circumlocutory discussion.

'One cannot stand with both, of course, and hence the tension the play breeds between opposing camps, viewing it as either satire or sexism. Hence, I stand with Kate but the play's *author*, who happens to be *Christopher Marlowe*, stands with Petruchio.' He smiles at me knowingly.

'Did you say *Marlowe*? Are you telling me Christopher *Marlowe* wrote "The Shrew?"' I stammer, incredulous, unsure if I've heard him correctly.

'Christopher Marlowe wrote "The Taming of the Shrew." I merely put my name to it. Marlowe is the true author,' Shakespeare declares in all calmness, despite the bombshell he's just dropped.

'Marlowe *wrote* "The Shrew,"' I repeat, finding it difficult to believe what I've just heard. Shakespeare coolly nods his head in the affirmative.

This is truly incredible. A bombshell. William Shakespeare did *not* write "The Shrew." But then another thought suddenly pops into my head, a thought that is altogether more consequential, something that is nothing less than earth shattering: if William Shakespeare didn't write "The Shrew," then what *else* didn't he write? Is the whole of Shakespeare's work – the greatest works ever written in the English language, maybe in any language – all to the credit of Marlowe and maybe others too? Was he merely the front man that allowed a true literary genius to work anonymously in the shadows?

That shadowy author variously attributed by Anti-Stratfordian scholars and sleuths to be either Sir Francis Bacon; Edward de Vere, 17th Earl of Oxford; William Stanley, 6th Earl of Derby; or...Christopher Marlowe. My head is spinning at the significance of those careless words just uttered by the Bard. That implausible but momentous sentence echoes in my head – "Christopher Marlowe wrote the Taming of the Shrew" – leaving me both giddy and on the brink of breaking one of the twenty first centuries most explosive stories!

Shakespeare smiles at me mischievously. He's enjoying my very obvious confusion. 'And yes, before you ask, '"The Shrew" was the only play, indeed the only work, that I didn't write. The reason I came to put my name to one of Marlowe's plays – as I'm sure you're curious to know – was simply down to misfortune –

his misfortune. Marlowe was a better playwright than he was a man of commerce – although he wasn't the best playwright either' – he smiles condescendingly – 'racking up some sum of considerable debts that I rather foolishly ended up bailing him out of. All he had for collateral was this semi-completed manuscript, really no more than a dog-eared thing, called "The Rape of the Shrew." This, he ended up forfeiting when he couldn't repay his debts to me.

'I refashioned it somewhat, tinkered around the edges here and there, changed the original title – which was a little too confronting even for an Elizabethan audience – then put it on the stage. Not one of my best productions, but good enough to repay capital and interest,' he smiles with a look of satisfaction.

'And you're absolutely certain, you can state categorically here and now, that this was the only work bearing your name *not* written by you?'

'Yes, yes, absolutely. Don't work yourself into a lather over it. There's nothing more to it than that.'

'But why now? Why reveal this…this bombshell *here* and *now*?' I persist.

'Well, when the oyster's ready to open…' he replies breezily, crossing his legs.

I'm finding it hard to share his nonchalance. Even if it's only the one play written by someone else's quill, that in itself is enough to rewrite literary history!

'Let's move on shall we,' he suggests with a hint of impatience, staring at the clock, clearly refusing to acknowledge the significance of his revelation, or at least giving that impression.

'Okay. Well let's do that,' I reply, trying to keep my voice steady despite the turmoil inside, while snatching a glance at my Sony UX570 recorder to make sure I've got all this on tape to dissect later.

I clear my throat and take a quick look at my notes to reorient myself. 'Let's move on then, from the past to the present. As you may know, your works are still considered relevant to this day as a means of reflecting upon and interpreting political and societal events.'

He dips his head slightly in acknowledgement.

'So, when you look at the world today, what parallels do you see with the times that you lived and wrote in?' I suddenly stifle an urge to sneeze. Hopefully not COVID given there's a seasonal spike thanks to the new variant doing the rounds.

'Hmm, well where to start?' He stares at me, narrowing his eyes and furrowing his brow. 'That's a very open-ended question with a world of possibilities.'

He makes a fair point. 'Okay, well let's start with politicians then, given some of the seismic shifts we're seeing in global politics today,' I suggest to help get the ball rolling.

Shakespeare pauses, gathering his thoughts before responding. 'The lust for power; the naked ambition to climb the greasy ladder and claim the crown; to command the attention of all other men; to be flattered and feted by high and low born alike; and to build a grand temple to the ego that all other men must worship at. These are the parallels between the prime ministers, presidents, dictators, and those who would be kings of your era and mine. Macbeth, the Henry's, and the Richard's are all echoes from the past that still ring loud today. Just as they did, your modern leaders connive, lie, cheat, and deceive their way to the top of the political dung heap, caring not whom they betray and harm in their relentless pursuit of power.

'And all to the worst of the fooled citizenry. However,' – he pauses – 'the princes, pretenders and perfumed potentates of my time sought not to wrap themselves in the false flags of patriotism, selflessness, high minded principles and betterment of the citizenry. No, they chose only the rank but honest odour of power and wealth. It seems to me, however, that today's politicians seek to dissemble and disguise their true motivations with their own sweet perfume. They fool the noses of good men with heady and beguiling scents, leading them like the Pied Piper to a promised land that is only a mirage, always just beyond reach, yet so enticingly close that they can almost taste its promise, almost feel it in their eager and deceived hands but never quite hold onto it. Everything has changed, yet nothing has changed! The state of Denmark still festers!' he exclaims, having worked himself up into quite a lather.

'I see, but isn't that a bit cynical?' I protest. 'Surely there are some politicians out there – decent men and women – pursuing agendas they genuinely believe in, thinking they will make the world a better place?'

'That is as maybe, but power is a tumour that corrupts even those pure of heart and purpose. "Decent men and women" may step onto the political ladder with noble intent but the higher they climb, the more their innocence is lost, until they reach the very top where the corruptive nature of power becomes irresistible. And, *even if* their intentions somehow remain noble, the inconsistencies and compromises demanded of high office create cynicism and a willingness to bend the rules: the means justifying the ends, the price being worth the paying. This moral corruption, once it gains a political toehold, spreads like a virus, like a coronavirus, until power for power's sake becomes the blind purpose: power is the opium of the politician!' Shakespeare declares, manifesting Marx with the zeal of a Bible waving preacher.

'So, if I understand you correctly and you view all forms of political leadership as inevitably immoral and corrupt, then what forms of government do you advocate? A people's commune in the merry fields of olde England, where all men are equal?' I challenge him.

'Hmm. You saw what happened after the people beheaded the Bourbon kings,' he retorts with a cynical sneer.

New boss, same as the old boss, I guess he means. A pox on all their houses. I shrug. Clearly, the Bard has a jaded – or astute – view of politics, which surprises me. But perhaps it shouldn't, given he's the author of some of the English language's most vivid portrayals of ambition, power, and corruption. His description of King Richard III as the "poisonous bunch-back'd toad," whose evil deeds in the quest for power matched only his grotesque appearance, comes to mind. I vaguely wonder to myself if King Richard was also fair-haired with an unruly thatch on top of his head?

'Politicians and politics are obviously timeless but so too are plagues and pestilence.' Shakespeare raises his eyebrows at this sudden conversational pivot. 'What I mean is we've had the Covid pandemic grip the world and disrupt our lives in ways we've never experienced before. But in many ways, this is old hat to a man of your era, and I can't help but thinking you've seen this all before. You're a man who tragically lost friends, fellow actors and close relatives – including your sisters and your son Hamnet – to the bubonic plague, the "Black Death." So, I'm sure you have some interesting insights and maybe even advice to share with us on how we face the next pandemic on this planet?'

The Bard stares at me, his face darkening. By the looks of him, I'm guessing I've rekindled the ashes of the past, of memories of fearful times when death stalked the streets of London and Stratford, randomly tapping victims on the shoulder and cruelly consigning them to the most awful of deaths from a disease so excruciatingly painful that it drove those infected to throw themselves from the roofs of buildings, seeking a merciful death below, as the buboes exploded inside their tormented bodies.

'They were the worst of times, dark and grim,' he begins in a sober tone. 'The harpies of hell all loosened upon the earth. No man knew when it would be his turn – the Grim Reaper's scythe hung over the heads of the healthy and living, as much as it did over the sick and dying. We had no science, no medicine, no knowledge to help us, only superstition, fear and loathing to guide us. The sick were quarantined in their homes, red crosses painted upon their doors; public gatherings were prohibited, *even* the theatres were closed – can you believe it? Travelers were forbidden from entering or leaving the city; neighbours fought neighbours to secure daily bread; and strangers, especially foreigners were cursed and shunned, as if they were the Devil himself.

'It was said you could contract the plague just by looking at a sick man, let alone sharing the same foul air as him. Everyone became suspicious and begrudging of everyone else; friends became foes; husbands and wives became cold bedfellows; the very fabric of community was frayed and torn by the hands of fear and ignorance. So, you ask me what parallels can be drawn between then and now? I say to you none that have any meaning! And feel lucky, feel very lucky, for that. In fact, run out into the streets and rejoice singing hallelujah and embracing the miracle of the modern times you live in, knowing that only a one hundredth of your sick will die, not one third of your entire population; knowing that your physicians will give you curative medicine if you're sick, not cut open your veins and bleed you to death; knowing that your plague can be studied under a microscope, not remain anonymous on the back of a rat; knowing what I have told you, that you can dispel your own fears and ignorance and hold onto your sanity. So, shall I stop there?'

He glares at me, chin jutting out and arms folded tightly across his chest, clearly agitated by his memories. Obviously, this is a topic that cuts too close to the bone for the Bard, and I can understand why – his own son, after all....

I notice the time. We're getting close to the end, and there's a lingering question that has played on my mind since the beginning of our conversation; a question that was earlier dismissed with an angry outburst. I clear my throat and prepare to return to the fray.

'If I can take you back to our earlier discussion about your portrayal of Shylock, emphasizing him as a figure beyond his religion, a symbol of religious tolerance perhaps. You hinted, or rather explicitly stated, that there was more to the story than meets the eye...' I pause here, uncertain how he will react given his previous outburst when I pushed him.

Shakespeare rolls his eyes and studies me for a few moments with sharp eyes, before responding in a measured tone. 'As you wish. Like all good tales, there's a dark secret with a sting in its tail. A secret that gathered dust in the rafters of Henley Street, our family home, for generations. Intrigued?' He raises his eyebrows at me. 'This secret was only revealed by chance, when my son Hamnet – may he rest in peace – was rummaging around in the attic and dislodged a parcel from the rafters. Inside that parcel was a collection of family heirlooms, including, to my surprise,' he pauses, 'pages from the Torah, in Hebrew, and a small Menorah.' He looks at me, expecting my response.

'Pages from the *Torah*? What were *they* doing in your roof?' I ask, surprised

'I don't know, you tell me, but there is one possibility, is there not?'

'Which is?'

Which is, that my forebears were practicing Judaism in secret.'

'Your ancestors were *Jewish*? Is that what you're trying to tell me?' Revelation upon revelation in this conversation!

'It's possible, is it not? How else do you explain those *things*,' he replies in a matter-of-fact way.

'Did you try and dig deeper, to find anything else that may have supported this, uh, *possibility*?'

'No,' he replies flatly.

'And why not? I'm sure I would have, I'm sure most people would have.'

'Because I did not,' he states firmly.

'Hmm, I see,' I reply diplomatically, wanting to avoid another flare up. 'Well, this certainly casts a whole new light on how we read Shylock in The Merchant of Venice, doesn't it.'

The Bard smiles enigmatically at me. I'm tempted to ask him why he's sharing this information only now and with me, but I sense he's not in a mood to entertain this topic for much longer and besides – I glance at the time – there's one final question I need to squeeze in. This one will be interesting. I glance at my notes scribbled on the last few pages of my "The Oxford Companion to Shakespeare."

'I'd like to close our conversation by touching on one of the greatest mysteries surrounding your life, if I may.'

'And what's that?' he asks, raising his eyebrows.

'Your death.'

'My death!' he snorts. 'What about my death?'

'Well, erm, how do I put this delicately? I guess I can't so here goes: how did you die? It's err, actually still a mystery that puzzles historians to this day.'

He snorts again, turning his face away from me, inadvertently exposing his neck. And then the penny drops! The answer is staring me in the face, quite literally! I take a longer closer look and yes, the answer is there! The scars on his neck, especially around the lymph glands, faded by the centuries but still visible, are symptomatic of the egg sized buboes that must have burst through his skin, causing it to rip and tear and leave behind those indelible marks. William-no-middle-name-Shakespeare died of the Black Death! A plague that scourged the land, from top to bottom, from town to country leaving no place safe. A plague that not satisfied with taking his sisters, his brother and even his own son, finally came for William Shakespeare, bringing down the curtains on one of the most epic and creative literary lives ever known to man.

A prosaic ending then. A death that grimly declined to imitate his art, instead mocking the tragic and complex endings that the Bard artfully devised for his own characters – such are the banalities of life. My mind darts to the Bard's final resting place, the Holy Trinity Church in Stratford upon Avon, which I recently visited as part of my research, and the enigmatic epitaph above his grave. As if reading my mind, he turns his face back to me, looks me squarely in the eyes, smiles, and then recites the last verse he ever wrote, the cursed verse that to this day protects his mortal remains – or so they say:

'"Good friend for Jesus' sake forbear,
To dig the dust enclosed here:
Blest be the man that spares these stones,
And curst be he that moves my bones."'

A CONVERSATION WITH LEONARDO DA VINCI

'So, why did you do it?' I ask, locking eyes on him.

Da Vinci shuffles in his seat, his body visibly tense, eyes dart furtively from side. 'It was either Giuliano or me. I know that sounds harsh, but I really had no choice. Believe me, I bore the Medici no ill will, none whatsoever. After all, they were patrons of the arts; they took me into their court and not just as a painter, but as an advisor, even a confidante. But as long as Giuliano lived, my life was in danger. I would have constantly looked over my shoulder, perpetually on tenterhooks, dreading the knock on the door from the Ufficiali di Notte – the Officers of the Night – to be hauled out of bed and dragged to the Palazzo della Signoria to face the Inquisitors, or' – he pauses, half-whispering – 'much worse.'

'But what did Giuliano Medici do to you that was so terrible, that would cause you to take such a drastic, some may even say, murderous course of action?' I ask, surprised by how worried, even scared, Da Vinci looks even after the passage of all this time.

'It was *he*, Giuliano di Lorenzo de' Medici, that accused me of doing that, that *thing*. It was *he* who placed the accusation against me inside The Tamburo. I know it!' he replies, the emotion high, his voice almost trembling.

'"The Tamburo?"' I ask puzzled, being unfamiliar with the term.

He harrumphs. 'Yes, The Tamburo! That uniquely Florentine mockery of justice, literally a box in front of the Palazzo della Signoria where anyone could anonymously – yes, *anonymously* – drop a written accusation against anyone else. It was no more than a means of settling personal scores and destroying the reputations and lives of good men and women. That letter box of defamation and damnation!' Da Vinci spits, now worked up into quite a lather.

'But what did Giuliano, golden boy of the Medici family, accuse you of that was so heinous?' I ask, referring to Giuliano's gilded reputation as the charming and athletic lady's man, who co-ruled Florence alongside his brother Lorenzo.

Da Vinci pauses, visibly straining to bring his emotions under control; I can see old wounds are being painfully picked open here. He composes himself before continuing then recites the following by rote, in a deadpan, almost magisterial voice: '"Leonardi di ser Piero da Vinci, amongst a company of indecent artists, was party to acts of perversion and moral debasement that sets himself against the laws of God and Man, by engaging on multiple occasions in acts of wickedness and depravity with the infamous artist's model and male prostitute known as Jacopo d'Andrea Saltarelli. For the good of public morality and to uphold the virtuous name of the Republic of Florence and to maintain the grace of God, I petition the court to proceed with all haste to open an investigation into said Leonardi di ser Piero da Vinci."'

He pauses and raises his head, glaring at me belligerently, as if I were his accuser. '*This* was the accusation written by the so-called "golden boy" Giuliano de' Medici and dropped anonymously into the Tamburo.' He crosses his arms, fuming.

'But did anyone take this accusation seriously? Were you arrested, for instance?'

'Arrested! Was I arrested?' he explodes, lunging forward in his seat, red eyed and looking a little wild. 'I was dragged out of Verrocchio's studio and hauled through the streets of Florence like some common criminal. I was thrown into a cell of such squalor and foulness that even the rats disdained it. Have you ever spent time in a Florentine prison cell, hmm?' he asks belligerently, jabbing his forefinger at me. 'Well, I can tell you, there is no man who embraces his liberty more than a man who's been trapped in such a place *and* has lived to see the sun again.'

He wipes his mouth on the back of his sleeve before continuing. 'But it was all lies, complete lies! Nothing but a malicious fabrication. There was not a shred of evidence presented, not one witness turned up in court to support the accusation, let alone the accuser himself. There was nothing other than that bilious piece of parchment and the inquisitors had no case to prosecute; no other choice but to declare me innocent – as much as it pained them to let anyone with a whiff of immorality walk free.'

I can see Da Vinci's sense of injustice and outrage still burns strong to this day, and I guess I can understand why, given the blight such an accusation would have had on the young artist's reputation in a society obsessed with sexual morality and religious piety.

'Guiliano didn't show up in court, even after he'd accused you, albeit anonymously, through the Tamburo?' I ask surprised.

'He was smarter than that. He didn't need to show his hand. The insinuation of immorality was almost as good as proof of immorality, thanks to the unique perversion of The Tambour system – which guaranteed any accusations would be investigated by the Court,' Da Vinci replies, flicking his thick curly locks from his face. 'But the damage was done. The taint of the accusation became a stain on my character. That, in essence, is the perversity of The Tambour – a platform for anonymous slander that costs the slanderer nothing but costs the accused everything. Florentine justice!' he scoffs bitterly.

'So, then that begs the question: how do you know Guiliano de' Medici was your accuser, if his identity was kept anonymous? How can you be so sure it was him?'

'Oh, I can be very sure it was him. Without a shadow of doubt,' retorts Da Vinci, rolling his eyes.

'How so?' I insist.

'Because of the evidence of my own eyes and ears,' he responds somewhat truculently.

'Okay, but what does that mean?' I insist again.

Da Vinci snorts. 'I knew Jacopo d'Andrea Saltarelli, many painters knew Saltarelli. He was a male model well known in the studios of Florence. He modelled at Verrocchio's – Andrea del Verrocchio, that is, the leading artist of the day, with whom I collaborated and was apprenticed to many years earlier – and even sat for me on occasion. He was attractive and charismatic in an impish sort of way, and of course, well, we all knew that he had more than one trick up his colourful sleeve. I also had an acquaintance with Guiliano de' Medici, be it as my client, my patron – no more than that,' he quickly adds.

'He commissioned me to paint his portrait around this time, but he was a terrible subject, always more interested in banter and small talk, rather than sitting still and getting the job done – he was a vacuous sort of fellow really, despite his golden image. Anyway, the portrait required a third sitting, which he demanded to have in the evening. This was both a surprise *and* a problem, given the dim lighting casts flickering shadows and creates a "halo noir" around the subject's head, making it the worst time of day for portraiture. Nevertheless, the patron pays the bills,' he sighs, sounding professionally aggrieved.

'However, rather than finding Guiliano ready for his sitting, I found him, how should I say, erm, in a *compromising position* with Jacopo Saltarelli, much to my horror!' Da Vinci flushes red. 'Neither he, nor Jacopo, seemed too concerned that I'd caught them in the middle of, erm, *the act*. In fact, almost the opposite: Guiliano seemed to get a perverse pleasure from being discovered like that.' Da Vinci shivers involuntarily, clearly revulsed at the memory. 'Needless to say, I didn't return to Palazzo Medici to finish the commission.'

He pauses. 'However, that wasn't the end of it. Guiliano turned up several times afterwards at Verrocchio's studio, but I always made myself scarce and kept out of his way, except...' He pauses again, longer this time, as if debating whether to tell me something. '...Except on one occasion, he managed to, erm, corner me.'

'Corner you?' I echo, surprised.

'Yes, corner me. He'd turned up late at night, almost materialized out of the gloom, smelling of wine. He was stumbling and obviously drunk. But it soon became clear why he was there because he, err,' – He clears his throat, squirming in his chair – 'erm, tried to force himself upon me, as if I was some tavern whore!' he exclaims in disgust. 'But I pushed him away, forcefully. He lost his footing and fell, which must have seriously bruised his ego even more than his backside, because he let forth a tirade of foul abuse that followed me out onto the street, including threats to my life,' Da Vinci states, with a mixture of anger and revulsion on his face.

'So, you're telling me Guiliano de' Medici, co-ruler of Florence and heir to the Medici fortune, tried to...seduce you?' I ask, incredulous. I mean, I know Guiliano's reputation as a playboy, and Da Vinci's noted good looks in his earlier years, but still, this is quite a twist in the tale!

'Well, I guess that's one way to put it,' he scoffs. 'It wasn't a pleasant experience. I can assure you. And crossing swords with a Medici, whatever the circumstances, was a dangerous thing for any man, let alone a common man: "Hell hath no fury like a Nobleman scorned" and that was particularly true of a Medici – as events would soon prove.' He sighs deeply, shaking his head.

'So that's when this whole business with The Tamburo started?'

'Yes, soon after.'

'But the court cleared you, right?'

'Yes, but that wasn't the end of it. Worse was yet to come.'

I raise my eyebrows as Da Vinci looks despondent.

'A month after the court issued its finding, I received an anonymous death threat, actually more of a death *warrant*. I was left with no illusions that Guiliano was behind it and that I was in mortal danger. Jacopo confirmed as much to me in a fit of remorse a few days later: you see, Guiliano had confided in him, on the other side of the pillow. It was inevitable, or so it seemed, that I'd end up with my throat cut, floating face down in the Arno – in those days assassins came cheap and life was even cheaper,' he says, sighing again, his face etched with worry. 'So, I was cornered. I was an artist from the hills facing the wrath of a Medici prince – can you imagine? Even fleeing Florence and going into self-exile provided no guarantee of safety as the Medici's influence spread across the length and breadth of Italy. Living a life of sleeping with one eye open; seeing assassins in every face in the crowd; descending into neurosis and terminal anxiety beckoned – no, that was not an option for me. The only way was to bring things to an outcome, way one or the other,' he says grimly.

'Bring things to an *outcome*? How did you propose to do that, given the odds were so stacked against you?'

'Ironically, the times favoured me. We lived in an age of upheaval and revolt. The Medici's wealth and power bred envy and hatred amongst their enemies – and they had many. Chief amongst them were the Pazzi, a family of proud and noble origins that traced their ancestry to a Knightly order that was the first to scale the walls of Jerusalem during the Crusades – or so they said,' he adds cynically. 'To them, the Medici's were common upstarts, outsiders, grubby money men who had amassed their banking wealth at the expense of the Pazzi's and used it to buy themselves respectability. The Pazzi's hatred for the Medici was a bottomless well of poison. So, you see, it wasn't too hard to find powerful people itching to bring things to a head with Guiliano.' Da Vinci's face has now hardened, his jaw set and lips pressed into a thin line. The cold intensity of this expression is both surprising and unsettling.

'So how did you recruit the Pazzi to your cause?' I ask, wondering how the bastard son of a Notary from an obscure hamlet in the Tuscan hills could convince the flower of Florentine nobility that he had something of value to offer them in their deadly feud with the Medici.

Da Vinci strokes his chin. He looks thoughtful, almost reflective, as he fixes me with his pale blue eyes, still radiating intensity and energy despite the passage of time. 'It's not something I'm particularly proud of. I know what you're thinking.

History likes to paint me as this virtuous, slightly eccentric polymath who disdained meat and rescued animals, and I suppose I was. But as I've said before, I was cornered and trying to survive. I had no recourse to force of arms; my only weapon was my intellect. So, to answer your question directly: I didn't recruit the Pazzi myself, I wasn't on personal terms with them. But, as is often the way, I knew someone who knew them – an introduction was arranged.'

'And who was this *someone* that arranged the introduction for you?'

'You probably know the name, at least by association with his better-known son – a family name that is synonymous with political intrigue and cynicism,' he replies, leaving the identity of his confederate hanging in the air.

'And that was who?'

'Bernardo di Niccolo Machiavelli,' he replies slowly.

'Machiavelli!' I exclaim, taken aback. 'You mean the author of "Il Principe?"' I know the name well – as we all do – and his infamous book – "The Prince," in English – the political treatise that remains to this day the ultimate guide on seizing and maintaining power through cunning and ruthlessness.

'No, no,' Da Vinci corrects quickly. '*That* Machiavelli was only nine at the time and several decades away from writing "The Prince." I'm referring to his father *Bernardo*. I knew him through artistic circles and occasionally tutored his son, Niccolo, the future author – a terrible painter by the way,' he adds as an aside. 'Bernardo and I got on well. He had his own problems with the Medici, as it turned out, so made a natural ally. In fact, my, erm, predicament seemed to galvanize him, almost injecting him with a sense of purpose, a zeal which took me by surprise. To be honest, I was expecting his counsel rather than his connivance in my cause. But then, that's the polarizing nature of the Medici's for you I guess.'

'What were *his* issues with the Medici?' I ask, curious.

'Bernardo's forebears were from a minor noble Florentine family, and he was set for great things in life – he was one of the youngest Doctor of Law and the best jurisprudence mind of his generation. However, sadly for him, his ambitions were thwarted by debts he'd inherited from his father and uncle – debts that prohibited him from going to the bar.'

'And what's that got to do with the Medici's?' I ask.

'You see, the debt he inherited was owed to the Medici and despite numerous requests was never forgiven by them. He was also associated with the Pazzi's via marriage and shared with his in-laws a common lifelong grudge against the Medici. And so now, Bernardo and I shared a common enemy. He concluded that the best course of action was to remove the Medici – I mean Guiliano – with the help of the Pazzi. At the beginning, they were distinctly unimpressed with our entreaties to them, dismissive in fact.

'As you said, what could we offer them? Bernardo was persuasive though, silver tongued – ever the barrister – and completely focused on drawing them into a conspiracy. Ultimately, he played on their political paranoia. He convinced them that the Medici were plotting to wipe them out, as part of a final solution to crush all political opposition and consolidate their grip on power, as well the Florentine banking system. The Pazzi, therefore, needed to act first, and fast. Actually, as it transpired there were solid kernels of truth in all of this – the Medici were on the warpath – which helped to add credibility to Bernardo's arguments. So maybe we just hastened the inevitable,' he adds, as if seeking to lessen his culpability in the bloodshed that was soon to follow.

'Okay, so Bernardo succeeds in playing on the Pazzi's justified insecurities, I get that. But how could you *actually* help them remove the Medici? I mean, forgive me for saying this, but you were just two men with a paint brush and a dodgy doctorate, so what did either of you have to offer them in a *practical* sense?' That was a tad caustic, I know.

Da Vinci narrows his eyes and glares at me. 'What you don't understand is that the threat of assassination always hung over the great and good of Florence in those days, whether Medici, Pazzi or Baroncelli. As a consequence, they always wore stiff leather undergarments to ward off the assassin's blade and as an added precaution, never stuck to a predictable schedule, making them hard to assassinate, especially a Medici. Guiliano and his brother Lorenzo were the wiliest of them all. They'd escaped numerous assassination attempts and were said to possess a sixth sense.

'So, how to get a Medici prince to walk into a trap? They were far too smart to accept an invitation to dinner from the Pazzi or any of their allies,' he says with a hint of sarcasm. 'No, it required someone who was known to the Medici, someone whom they trusted or at least saw as safe, even harmless, to encourage them into a place and time of the Pazzi's choosing.'

'And that's where you came in, I assume?' I ask as the penny starts to drop.

He grinds his teeth and sucks in air. 'You could say I was the bait in a "Machiavellian" trap. Not a role I volunteered for, I hasten to add. More a case of Bernardo tactically manoeuvring me into a position that I couldn't back out of,' he laments.

'Father like son: intrigue obviously ran deep in their family blood,' I observe.

'More than you know,' he replies tellingly. 'But the trap thus baited would deliver the hunter to the hunted and the tables would turn. And the plan was simple, actually. All I had to do was entice Guiliano to a meeting on the pretext of hearing my plea for mercy, to spare my life and then the Pazzi's men would, well, take care of the rest.' He smiles sheepishly.

'And how did you intend to entice him to meet with you, I mean without endangering yourself?' I ask.

'Again, that wasn't difficult. I reached out to Jacopo, ever pliant and asked him to arrange a meeting, to which the reply quickly came back in the affirmative. I guess Guiliano couldn't believe his luck, or my stupidity, because from his perspective I was the one walking into a trap. He had no intention of parlaying with me and had only murder on his mind.'

'Seems all too simple, doesn't it? I mean, the Medici

princes had antennas finely tuned to danger, and there you were ostensibly presenting yourself to Guiliano on a platter,' I challenge him.

'Yes, you're right, of course the man was no idiot. The plan was to lure Guiliano to the supposed safe ground of Verrocchio's studio, straight after Sunday mass. However, we got word from Jacopo early that morning that Guiliano had got cold feet and wasn't going to show up himself – instead he was going to send his henchman.'

'The best laid plans of men and mice,' I reply wryly.

'Indeed, but there was no turning back at that point, we'd all come too far, we were all too exposed. "By the grace of God, the Medicis must die today."'

I sit upright in my chair, taken aback by his cold callous words, while Da Vinci regards me with his sharp, intelligent eyes.

'Those were Francesco de' Pazzi's words, not mine,' he clarifies for my benefit. 'He was incensed, seething in fact, that Guiliano had slipped through his fingers again and was determined to finish the job that morning. After a heated debate, he and the other leaders of the conspiracy – Bernardo Baroncelli and Francesco Salviati – took their men and hurried off straight to the Duomo, where we learnt both Medici brothers were attending High Mass.'

'You mean they intended to assassinate Guiliano in the cathedral, at prayer?' I ask, alarmed.

'Yes, I know how abhorrent that sounds. Machiavelli advised them against it – if nothing else, it risked turning the people against them. But they did it anyway, all hot-headed, driven by the scent of blood, I guess.' He pauses, his face cast downward. 'But that wasn't the worst of it; when they reached the Duomo, things went from bad to worse.'

'What do you mean, from "bad to worse?"'

'You see, the Pazzi's quickly got to Guiliano in the cathedral. It was all too easy really. He went down under a flurry of blades. Baroncelli and Franceso led the attack. Guiliano lay there in a pool of blood, a look of shock on his face – I'll never forget that look. They then instantly turned on Lorenzo, like a pack of dogs – it was the unkindest of cuts.' He falters, biting his nails, as if still in shock at the bloodshed that greeted his eyes in the Duomo on that fateful Sunday morning in April 1478. 'And that wasn't part of the bargain! That wasn't the plan. We'd only ever talked about assassinating Guiliano, removing him as a mutual threat. Never once did we discuss, let alone agree, to killing Lorenzo, or anyone else,' he complains, his face looking ashen and his body hunched.

I regard him, letting his words sink in. *Something doesn't sound quite right here*, I think to myself. I search his face: does he protest too much? How can he have not known – or at least considered the possibility – that the conspirators were aiming for a wholesale slaughter of the Medici, especially in the heat of the moment with the red mist clouding their eyes? Surely their whole raison d'etre was regime change, a coup d'etat and let's be honest, they were never in it to fix Da Vinci's problems. I slowly shake my head in disbelief.

'Are you seriously telling me that you had no inkling of the broader plot to wipe out the Medici? You, who were sitting so close to the centre of the conspiracy. You, who would have been privy to many of the plans and details?'

Da Vinci winces at my challenge and looks away. 'Of course I knew the Pazzi wanted Lorenzo out of the way. But I assumed they'd exile him, or something like that, not attempt to assassinate him! That's not something I could ever have gone along with. I'm not a murderer. I acted only out of self-defence. This was only ever about Guiliano and me. In fact, I was on friendly terms with Lorenzo, despite the, erm, challenges I had with his brother. He was a patron of the arts – he took personal interest in my work, both artistic and scientific. I never would have meant him any harm.'

I arch my eyebrows.

'When I saw what was happening in the cathedral, when I processed the awful truth, I rushed to Lorenzo's side along with the poet Poliziano and Francesco Nori – who took a deadly blow for Lorenzo – and helped shield him until we gained safety in the sacristy. And I stayed by his side, until the very end, until we were sure the tide had turned, and the Pazzi plot had been rolled back by the Medici loyalists.'

I'm incredulous at what I'm hearing! I can't believe it: one minute he's the co-conspirator hurrying to the Duomo to do harm to Guiliano de' Medici, and the next, he's rushing to the aid of his brother Lorenzo, to shield him from the very same co-conspirator's knives. The gall of the man! I pause to find the right words to respond and then lean forward fixing Da Vinci with a glare.

'So, you're telling me, in a split second, you decided to turn your back on your fellow plotters and made good with the Medici camp, all the while knowing Guiliano was dead, lying in a pool of blood, the threat to your life removed? Do you know how extraordinary that sounds? Surely there's more to this than you're telling us, there's more to your involvement in the plot?'

Da Vinci looks at me sheepishly, physically squirming in his chair. 'As I said, I had no knowledge of the larger plot – the Pazzi's plans to overthrow the Medici. They didn't bring me, or Bernardo, for that matter, into their inner circle. Why would they? Who were we to them? You said it yourself. Call me naive if you will, but that's the truth. I had no grudge against the Medici...other than with Guiliano.'

'So that's it? You end up on the winning side, Guiliano removed, you looking like a hero and your co-conspirators dead – all of them rounded up and summarily executed within days – leaving no one alive to implicate you. All very neat and tidy, wouldn't you say?' I exclaim, with a dose of cynicism, struggling to understand whether this was a selfless act triggered by genuine concern for a patron and friend, as events rapidly spun out of control beyond his expectations, *or* the quick-witted actions of a turncoat who suddenly sensed that the day would eventually be won by the Medici.

'I understand how it might seem to you, but it wasn't like

that, not at all. It wasn't all so neatly tidied up and forgotten; my life was still in danger,' he pleads, spreading his arms out in protest. 'After the initial bloodshed, the Medici meticulously turned over every stone, hunting down anyone with even the slightest hint of involvement in the plot – a true witch hunt! And that's when they arrested Bernardo. He was brutally tortured but didn't betray me, even though my name was on a list they demanded he denounce. Jacopo was also hauled in and beaten but didn't give me away either, much to my surprise. However, it was very clear that I was under suspicion. It felt like it was only a matter of time until it was my turn – the sword of Damocles hanging over me once again.' He sighs.

'So, how did you get away with *your* head, when so many others were arbitrarily strung up from the Palazzo della Signoria?' I demand to know.

'Lorenzo, of course,' he replies, looking embarrassed. 'He shielded me from the inquisitors. He either didn't – or didn't want to – believe suspicions of my involvement. I suppose after all I'd done for him, it was hard for him to think otherwise.'

'You mean your *timely* intervention on his behalf in the Cathedral?'

'That, yes.' Da Vinci pauses for a few moments, looking reflective, before continuing. 'However, no man can truly ever escape his past.' He looks up at me, almost plaintively. 'Over time the whispering, the rumours, got to such a point that Lorenzo could no longer ignore suspicions of my guilt. He had to be seen to act, or else risk his own credibility. Behind his back they even started to call him "Lorenzo the Manipulated." And then there were those in court who were envious of my influence with him, including Poliziano the poet, ironically. I had to leave Florence, leave Lorenzo's court, both for his sake and mine.

'If truth be told, I was living a lie anyway. I who was instrumental, albeit unwittingly, in attempting the downfall of the Medici; the murder of Guiliano; and all the strife that followed, living and working in the Medici court as an artist, a trusted friend, a "hero" who helped save the prince from the assassins' blades – it was all a fraud. No, it was time to leave Florence, possibly forever. Lorenzo protested of course, perhaps too much... perhaps deep down he knew, or had his suspicions, that I was his brother's murderer. But we'll never know. It was twenty years, twenty long years, before I finally returned to Florence, and by then, he was dead.'

Da Vinci comes to a sudden stop, and looks down at the floor, his long locks falling forward, as an air of melancholy descends on the room. He gently rubs his eyes, which are by now moist.

I look away and turn to my side, picking up my copy of "The Life Of A Renaissance Master" by Giorgio Vasari, turning the last page in the tumultuous chapter titled "First Florentine Period (1472 to c.1482)." I then flick forward and glance at my notes in the following chapter: "First Milanese Period (c.1482 to 1499)."

I noisily clear my throat, causing Da Vinci to look up at me. 'From Florence to self-exile in Milan, to focus your career on the design and manufacture of novel weapons of destruction, serving some of Italy's most ambitious and warlike lords and princes – a new chapter in life as Italy's Master of Arms,' I state.

Da Vinci stares at me with a mixture of puzzlement and alarm, shaking his head. 'No, no, that's a misrepresentation, an exaggeration,' he remonstrates. 'I offered my services to Ludovico Sforza, Duke of Milan, as a weapon designer, yes, but also as an engineer of novel scientific and mechanical devices, as well as a master painter. It's true to say that I had designs that could give him an edge on the battlefield – surely an advantage to any ruler harried by the French, like he was – but,' he pauses, looking rueful, 'he kept me on more for his own pleasure and entertainment. At the end of the day, he was more interested in frippery and baubles than science and advancement. He was no Lorenzo; not a man of refinement and learning at all. He was rather boorish actually, more, how would you say, "nouveau riche."'

He wrinkles his nose in obvious distaste. 'He had me wasting my time designing mechanical toys and party tricks for the amusement of his vacuous guests. Quite possibly the worst employer I ever had,' he harrumphs.

'But on the other hand, didn't you produce some of your greatest works of art under his patronage?' I try to correct him.

'For example?' he sniffs.

'For example: "Lady with an Ermine;" "The Last Supper;" and "The Virgin of the Rocks."

He harrumphs again. 'That's as maybe, but they were paintings, just paintings,' he responds testily. 'No more than bright fanciful things to please the dull eye and flatter the shallow ego of a deep purse. Sforza and his ilk didn't know their Michelangelo from their Botticelli,' he sneers.

I arch my eyebrows in surprise. "'*Just* paintings you say?'"

'Yes of course, I know you'll tell me how history looks upon these things as such wondrous expressions of renaissance art and so on. But to be brutally honest, painting bored me. It was tedious laborious work, constrictive of imagination and mind, nothing more than the instinctive movement of hand guided by the eye. To me, it was a means to an end, just a way to pay the bills, keep my patrons happy, and give me space to conduct my experiments. Honestly, most mornings I dreaded getting out of bed to face another day of tedium, staring at a half-finished picture while my wrist mechanically flicked up and down, captive to the canvas. But I tell you' – He leans towards me, looking me straight in the face, his eyes intense – 'the most soul destroying part of it all, the ultimate perdition, was those bloody church walls; blank canvases of mortar taunting me with their vast nothingness, their seemingly endless acreage that defied hope of ever covering them in paint before the madness of monotony took grip.'

Before I was surprised, but now, I'm shocked! I lean back and take a few moments to digest what I've just heard: unless I'm completely missing something here, Leonardo Da Vinci is telling me that one of history's most renowned artists had no more passion for his artwork than the teller at my local bank branch does for counting coins!

'Surely you must have been rewarded with *some* satisfaction, a sense of achievement even, once you finished your paintings and could reflect upon all their richness, the subtle capture of both the divine and human, if not just their sheer technical brilliance?' I half plead with him.

'In the early days, at Verrocchio's, maybe, probably. Mastering the technical composition and use of new materials satisfied my intellectual curiosity, to some extent. But my passion was always science, understanding how life around us works, how the human body functions, why birds can fly and so on. You've seen my drawings, my experiments on paper, they say it all, don't they?' he says emphatically.

'But I've also seen your paintings, they say something too, surely? Take "Lady with an Ermine" for example ...' I say, recalling my recently completed research trip to the Czartoryski Museum to view the original of the "Lady" – a portrait of Cecilia Gallerani, an undoubted beauty and favourite mistress of Sforza – and her pet ermine, a short-tailed weasel, with a nasty temper, sitting uncomfortably in her arms.

Da Vinci instantly glares at me with fire in his eyes, cutting me off mid-sentence: "Lady with a *bloody* Ermine!" he spits. 'That creature on her lap was nothing more than a vicious rat. Look! Look at this! See where it bit me!' he states angrily, thrusting his index finger at me to reveal a faint scar around the tip. 'And as for Cecilia Gallerani,' Da Vinci harrumphs, '"lady" is not a word I would choose to apply to that particular woman!'

'What do you mean by that?' I ask, taken aback by his sudden hostility.

'Well, let's just put it this way, she wasn't the most pleasant nor cooperative of subjects. And sitting for her portrait wasn't the only thing she had in her mind!' he sneers.

'Tell me more,' I exhort him, my curiosity pricked.

Da Vinci grunts, a mixture of anger and embarrassment on his face. 'I was there to paint her portrait and nothing more. But she had, erm, other ideas.'

'Other ideas?'

'Yes. She seduced me,' he replies reluctantly, shifting uncomfortably in his chair, his face reddening.

'*Seduced* you?' I echo in disbelief. 'How did that, err, happen?'

'She was cunning,' Da Vinci states with a sigh. 'She knew how to manipulate people. One evening, she called me into her chambers to discuss the portrait. She was unhappy with her nose, or some such nonsense. And before I knew it, she had me in a, erm, compromising position. And then Sforza walked in.'

'Sforza caught you?' I ask, leaning forward, almost feeling the unbearable awkwardness of the situation.

'Yes,' Da Vinci replies with bitterness in his voice. 'He was furious. Violent. Cecilia pleaded that I had tried to rape her. She played the victim perfectly. Sforza believed her, despite my protests and threatened to have me executed.'

'Executed?!' I echo, shocked. 'So, what did you do?'

'I had no choice,' he replies grimly. 'I approached Sforza's mercenaries in secret. They were unhappy with their pay and treatment. I convinced them that their best option was to desert and join the French forces advancing on Milan.' Da Vinci pauses, looking tense. 'I first approached Hans Müller, a Swiss mercenary, captain of the Reislaufer. He had shown an interest in some of my military designs and liked to paint a bit too. I also knew he was pragmatic. I appealed to his sense of self-preservation, pointing out Sforza's dwindling resources and the inevitability of defeat. Müller was sceptical at first, but the prospect of getting a better payout from the French and the growing discontent among the ranks swayed him – the Swiss are a very practical lot you know,' he adds.

'And it worked?' I ask.

'Yes.' Da Vinci nods. 'The mercenaries deserted Sforza on the eve of the Battle of Novara, in 1500. Without them, Sforza's forces were easily defeated by the French and Sforza was captured and imprisoned in France.'

'Where he died?' I ask. Da Vinci nods his head, looking away, avoiding eye contact with me.

'And Cecilia? What happened to her?'

'Well, she's still hanging around, isn't she?'

Was that an uncharacteristic attempt at humour, I wonder.

'Although, if you look closely at the right side of her mouth, in the corner,' he continues with a smug look on his face, 'you'll notice the slightest of supercilious sneers.'

Was this Da Vinci's immortal revenge on Cecilia?

I stay silent for a few moments, deep in thought and then look Da Vinci squarely in the eye. 'You see the parallels here, don't you? You must, right?' Da Vinci narrows his eyes at me, looking puzzled. 'First Guiliano, as well as nearly Lorenzo. And then Sforza. You were a mortal danger to patrons and princes. The most "Machiavellian" of Renaissance artists, whose prowess for conspiracy and subterfuge was as unrivalled as his paintings. You, Leonardi Da Vinci, were a very dangerous man to be around!' I exclaim.

Da Vinci blinks at me, wide eyed, clearly taken aback by my accusation. 'Me? Dangerous?' he stammers. 'I won't deny that sometimes my actions may have appeared to be, um, ruthless. But I've already explained that to you. I only did what I did to survive, to defend myself from princes and patrons. In those times, survival meant outsmarting those who held power over you. I had no sword, no shield, my only weapon was my intellect.'

He looks at me intently. 'You must understand, the Renaissance was not just a period of artistic and scientific flourishing; it was also a time of political intrigue and constant power struggles. Machiavelli's "Il Princip" was simply a reflection of the times. Navigating this world required more than just talent with a brush or a chisel. It demanded a sharp mind, a keen understanding of the baseness of human nature, and the ability to manoeuvre through the treacherous waters of court politics.' He pauses, his expression thoughtful. 'Every patron, every prince, every powerful figure I encountered had their own agenda. To survive, I had to be more than just an artist. I had to be a strategist, a diplomat, and yes, at times, a conspirator.'

I contemplate the wizened old man in front of me, ruminating on what he's just told me. His clear distaste for his own art, combined with his conspiratorial cunning, are both jarring and astonishing. It's not what any art historian would ever want to hear, nor indeed any casual admirer of his work, of which of course there are many. The reality of who the man really is, is a far cry from the image cherished by so many. But the truth is the truth, I guess. Maybe we expect too much of our icons and heroes, who after all are only the same mixed palette of frustrations, inadequacies and basic instincts as the rest of us.

'Maybe, I think, we should just keep this conversation to ourselves,' I tell him quietly. I glance again at my copy of "The Life of a Renaissance Master" and turn the pages. 'So, you finally left Milan and the patronage of Sforza after fifteen years – and I won't ask why you stuck it out for so long given your obvious distaste for him – to try your luck with Agostino Barbarigo, the Doge of Venice,' I state.

'Hmm. Sforza was his own worst enemy, more of an enemy than Louis XII. If he'd had the imagination, the daring, half a brain even, to put my weapon designs into practice the French wouldn't have taken Milan – regardless of the desertion of the Swiss. Instead, he preferred the amusement of mechanical floats and giant bronze horses, rather than the armoured vehicles and multiple launch artillery pieces I offered him.' Da Vinci harrumphs. 'The Doge however, now he was a man with imagination and strategic insight and understood the benefit science and innovation could bring to warfare. He offered me free reign as his military architect and engineer, giving me space to develop my designs, all intended to protect the Republic from Ottoman attack. It felt like meaningful work to me, it was a very satisfying period of my life,' he states with obvious satisfaction.

'But a very short period of your life,' I add.

'Yes, yes, all too short.' He sighs. 'The place was full of money lenders – the Venetians were a rapacious lot, you see – all too eager to extend a loan on the friendliest possible terms, but woe betide any man who fell behind on his re-payments.' Da

Vinci grimaces, turning over his hands and staring at them, as if to check they're still intact.

'You fell foul of the money lenders?' I quiz.

'The Doge was as tight fisted as he was wily, and I don't think I ever received payment other than board and lodging.' He laughs uncomfortably. 'And besides, I was a Florentine and after all those years in exile, it was time to go home and test the waters, see what had changed. And I had it on good authority that my return would be, erm, welcomed.'

'And were you? Welcomed back, I mean?'

'More or less, I suppose,' he replies, stroking his chin. 'I wasn't quite the house guest of the Medici, not straight away anyway, but I found hospitality at the monastery of Santissima Annunziata. And a studio.'

'The studio where you produced "The Virgin and Child with Saint Anne and Saint John the Baptist," a work that according to Vasari: "Men and women, young and old flocked to see it as if they were going to a solemn festival."'

'It was only a cartoon, a trivial thing, something to keep the monks amused. Don't overestimate it, please' he replies, sounding slightly annoyed.

Okay, as you wish, let's move swiftly on, I think to myself.

'It was also about this time that your rivalry with another master of the Renaissance took hold, was it not?' I state.

Da Vinci frowns at me, narrowing his eyes. 'You're referring to *vir musculorum*, aren't you?'

'"Vir musculorum?"' I echo, raising my eyebrows.

'It's Latin for muscle man,' he replies testily.

'You mean Michelangelo?'

'Indeed I do,' he replies, regarding me with a stony face.

'Why "muscle man?"' I ask, suppressing a smirk at the cute nickname.

'It's obvious, isn't it? His brawny drawings and sculptures, all sinews and muscles, bare buttocks, and erm, male appendages. All a bit too homo-erotic for my taste,' he replies dismissively, revealing a competitive streak – or is it a jealous streak?

That has hitherto been hidden from our conversation.

'Ah, I see,' I reply delicately.

'I on the other hand, focused on subtlety and the perfection of human anatomy,' he states rather haughtily. I can tell he's clearly miffed at even the mention of his former arch-rival, the "muscle man."

'It sounds like there were more than just artistic differences at play between the two of you – a strong personal animosity as well?'

'Hmm. Michelangelo was brash and arrogant, always eager to prove himself superior. A wild young man in a hurry.'

'Is it true, according to Vasari, that he often mocked your work, and in public too, calling it unfinished and overly meticulous? That must have been difficult to deal with.'

'What would you expect from a stone mason,' he harrumphs. 'There were times when I wanted to confront him directly, but I chose to let my work speak for itself.'

I suppress another smile: 'I've never heard of the preeminent sculptor of the Renaissance and creator of the sublime statue of David, belittlingly referred to as a "stonemason" before.'

'Did you ever have any direct confrontations with Michelangelo?'

'Oh, there were a few I suppose.'

'Do you care to expand?'

'If you insist. Take that overbearing statue of David, for example. I, along with others on the committee deciding what to do with it, believed it should have been placed in the Duomo or even Santissima Annunziata, as modesty dictated. But of course, Michelangelo insisted it be placed in front of the Palazzo Vecchio – the town hall – for all the world to see, a shining monument to his sublime brilliance. He stormed into the committee meeting, accusing me of trying to undermine him – utter nonsense, of course – and caused quite a ruckus, I can tell you. I distinctly recall Botticelli having to lead him out of the chamber,' he snorts. 'And, he had the temerity of accusing *me* of not being able to finish anything, pointing to my numerous *so-called* unfinished projects. I retorted, of course, by questioning his understanding of anatomy, which infuriated him!'

'That sounds intense. There were also rumours that Michelangelo had a secret plot against you. Is there any truth to that?'

Da Vinci sighs. 'Unfortunately, yes. He was infuriated when the Council of Florence decided to give both of us the commission to decorate the Hall of Five Hundred, in the Palazzo Vecchio. Personally, I had no problem with this, but of course he did. Eventually, after Botticelli interceded, he agreed to paint one side of the Hall if I stuck to the other. I started work on "The Battle of Anghiari" – the council insisted on a grand statement of Florentine glory, all propaganda of course – and he worked on "The Battle of Cascina." All well and good, or so you would think.

'However, Michelangelo was not above using underhanded tactics. He bribed one of my apprentices to sabotage my work on the mural. The apprentice tampered with the pigments, causing the colours to fade prematurely, completely ruining the work. An utter disaster, while muscle man sniggered from the other side of the Hall.'

Da Vinci looks furious, steam almost coming out of his ears.

'That's shocking! How did you handle the situation?'

'It was a difficult time for me, no doubt. My credibility was on the line, after all, I'd only recently returned to Florence. But in the end, I'm afraid to say, I had to abandon the mural – it was beyond salvage – and I left Florence for the second time,' he sighs deeply.

'Did you ever confront Michelangelo about this?'

'I did, of course I did, but he denied everything, as he would. And there was no evidence, even though I applied the thumb screws to my treacherous apprentice…metaphorically speaking, of course,' he quickly adds.

'Of course.' I smile.

'Well anyway, no smoke without fire and he hastily left for Rome without ever finishing his commission.'

'Looking back, do you have any regrets about how things unfolded between you two?'

'Perhaps, but I don't regret standing up for my artistic vision. Michelangelo and I were both passionate about our work, and that passion sometimes led to conflict. I suppose in hindsight his work had *some* artistic merit,' he admits grudgingly, 'but the man himself, well, I'm not sure, even now, I would apply the word merit to him,' he adds caustically.

Hmm, time is obviously not always a great healer, I reflect to myself. And talking of time – I glance at the clock – we're nearly out of it and there's one last enigma that's come down to us through ages, still intriguing millions to this day, that needs to be discussed: yes, that enigmatic smile!

'So, master Leonardo, there's one last thing. Something that's been puzzling me and many generations of art lovers. A puzzle that exercises academic minds to this day and continues to stir heated debate, and I'm hoping that you can help solve it once and for all.' Da Vinci cocks an eyebrow, indicating I've got his attention. '*Who* is the Mona Lisa?'

Da Vinci leans back in his chair and chuckles, giving me a knowing look. I think he was expecting this. 'The enigma of the Mona Lisa *is* the whole point of the Mona Lisa. Take a long critical look at the painting you see in the Louvre today; it's a workmanlike effort but nonetheless an unremarkable piece of Renaissance portraiture. Ask yourself this: does it have any greater artistic merit than say "The Doge" by Bellini; "La Schiavona" by Titian; or even let's say "Castiglione" by Raphael?' he asks rhetorically. 'No, I don't think so. It's just a product of its age, and in many ways those other portraits are far superior in their composition,' he adds modestly.

'But what intrigues every passing visitor in the Louvre who stares at her face, whether consciously or subconsciously, is the mystery of her identity. That is the essential pulling power of the Mona Lisa,' he states, a look of satisfaction spread across his face.

'Hmmm,' I absorb this piece of self-deprecation for a moment. 'But the slight curl of the lip and the entrancing eyes, aren't *they* the essence of the Mona Lisa?' I suggest.

'They're *just* facial features, human physiology, pure and simple, nothing more to it,' he replies directly.

'Okay,' I reply, sounding unconvinced. 'But even if that's so, you still haven't answered the question: "*who* is she?"' I persist.

Da Vinci's face darkens for a fleeting moment, only to be replaced by a cryptic smile and a hint of mischief in his eyes, as they lock on mine. He then slowly leans closer to me, in a conspiratorial way and says in a hushed voice, so close to my ear I can feel his breath.

'She is...me. She is...you. She is...everyone. But she is...no one.'

He pulls away and looks at me. The room seems to grow quieter, the air heavier with the weight of his revelation, if you can call it that. I sit back absorbing his words, not sure if they're just puff – bullshit even – or imbued with some meaning that I can't grasp, at least not in the moment. I scrutinize his face. It's almost expressionless, mildly enigmatic maybe, except for a slight curl of the lip and those entrancing pale blue eyes that seem to follow me as I get up to leave the room.

A CONVERSATION WITH JOHN FITZGERALD KENNEDY, 35TH PRESIDENT OF THE UNITED STATES

'Why did you do it?' I ask, leaning forward, locking eyes with him.

Kennedy shifts in his chair, straightening his perfectly knotted tie and chuckles in that evasive way politicians do when they're brushing off an uncomfortable question.

'Who could blame you? I mean *who* could have resisted her? I doubt I could have,' I continue, with a mix of flattery and contrived bonhomie, beaming at him knowingly. He just responds to me with a thin smile.

'Your brother Bobby certainly couldn't, could he? Resist her I mean,' I press, aiming to hit a nerve, playing on the rumour that his brother – ever the competitive one – had picked up where Kennedy left off.

Kennedy laughs dismissively. 'Bobby and Marilyn; Marilyn and Jack; Sinatra and Marilyn; Hoffa and Sinatra even; it's all just a merry go-round of rumour and gossip – take your pick, match your cards,' he replies, breaking his silence. He crosses his legs in his neatly pressed sharp-lined grey trousers and smiles at me, albeit a smile without warmth.

'It was a steamy birthday number she sang to you at Madison Square Garden though, wasn't it?' I suggest, recalling Marilyn Munroe's sultry, intimate rendition of "Happy Birthday to You," dressed in skin-tight, nude-coloured dress adorned with 2,500 rhinestones, adding to the allure of her performance. 'Almost an ode to raw sexual attraction, a verbal strip tease brazenly performed in front of New York's good and great. And not to mention poor Jacqui, standing there dutifully wearing the mask of first Lady and adoring wife, while wincing on the inside at the excruciating embarrassment of it all,' I state.

'Well, that was quite the performance. There's no denying that,' he exclaims, unable to resist a broad smile spreading across his face. 'Marilyn sure knew how to work a crowd. The truth is, though, she was probably as high as a kite – her party trick was knocking back cocktails of speed and booze. No doubt Sinatra or Crosby put her up to it – that was the sort of fooling around they got up to in those days – you know, the Rat Pack,' he laughs as if it was all just high jinks and chooses to deliberately ignore my pointed comment about Jackie.

'So, did you sleep with her? I mean that night in March '62 at Crosby's place, at the Rancho Mirage?' I ask pushing him, getting straight to the point, alluding to that infamous all-night party hosted by Bing Crosby that was rumoured to have brought Kennedy and Marilyn together.

Kennedy chuckles dismissively again. 'I told you, don't let yourself get fooled by all the rumours and gossip. The long and short of it is that we were both guests of Bing's that night. There was some socializing, there was always some socializing in those days, we had a good time, a very good time, that was it, no more no less. There's no story here, as much as you'd like one.' He leans his arm on the back of his chair, trying to look relaxed.

'Sounds like a wasted opportunity to me, what with that heady mix of booze, drugs, film stars, Presidents, maybe even a Mafioso or two. I'm sure one thing could have led to another, and the night could have ended with a bang, I mean a *big* bang,' I persist, smiling in an insinuating way.

'Don't waste your time Mister,' Kennedy responds, his piercing Irish eyes fixing me with a look.

'Okay, but there were *other* women though, weren't there?' I state, rather than ask, continuing to pull on the thread.

'There are always other women,' Kennedy replies dismissively.

'I mean women *other* than Jacqui.'

'I know what you mean,' he replies tartly.

'Do you recall the late British prime minister, Harold McMillan?'

Kennedy raises his eyebrows. 'Super Mac? Yeh, sure I do,' he replies breezily.

'Good. Then let me quote you *Super Mac*: "If I don't get laid at least once a day, I get a headache." I scan his face for a reaction.

'I didn't pick Harry as the randy type, more of a stiff upper lip Brit,' he responds with a chuckle, crossing his legs.

'Indeed,' I smile. 'But that was a quote from *you* to him, when he visited the Whitehouse, as told by the man himself, in April '62. And I love this one,' I continue, glancing at my research notes, 'from your special assistant Kenneth O'Donnell: "It appears to me that today most Americans suffer from over-consumption of hamburgers and fries, whereas our President is very mindful of his diet and only suffers from an overconsumption of women."'

Kennedy can't help smiling at that one, despite his attempts to stop himself.

'So how many women were there?' I persist.

'Oh dozens, at least one a day,' he replies facetiously, still deflecting.

'Interns, call girls, secretaries…' I suggest.

'You're a persistent sort of fellow, aren't you,' he replies.

I guess I am, I think to myself, seeing I'm getting under his skin.

'So, tell me about Judith Campbell, or Judith Exner as she later became. Did you love her, or were you just lovers?' I ask bluntly.

Kennedy lets out an exasperated sigh. 'Well, it's all there in black and white, in the Washington Post archives isn't it, so I guess it's no state-secret that Judith and I were *friendly* for a while,' he concedes.

'"Friendly,"' I repeat, arching my eyebrows.

'Yeh, you know, we were *friendly*. Frankie introduced us in

’60 in Las Vegas. I guess he had his ulterior motives – Frankie was like that, you know, always trying to connect people, always the chess player trying to create moves on the board, positioning pieces for when they might be useful later. Judith was different to any of the women I’d come across before: different to Gene, different to Ava and *very* different to Jacqui. Sure, she was stunningly beautiful, but she was more than that, she was exhilarating and unpredictable, even dangerous, like one of those white-knuckle rides at the fairground. We hit it off straight away and our friendship went from there,’ Kennedy replies, his expression and tone clearly conveying his affection and admiration for her.

‘A femme fatale maybe? A modern-day Mata Hari, according to some at the time.’

‘Yeh, I guess you could say that,’ he affirms casually.

‘How did Jacqui feel about it? I mean, she must have known what was going on, not just with Judith but with those wild pool parties at the White House and everything else. She even said as much to her press secretary, didn’t she? What was it?’ – I glance at my notes – ‘“I’m afraid to admit it but every poor young woman that opens that door to the Oval Office, inevitably ends up opening her legs to my husband.”’

Kennedy harrumphs, flashing me a glare. ‘Jacqui had Aristotle!’ he shoots back.

‘But “what’s good for the goose…”’ I respond, smiling, hinting at the double standards at play here.

Kennedy studiously ignores the comment.

‘Back to Judith. Were her links to the mafia, her relationship with Sam Giancana and John Roselli, part of the thrill, part of the ride too?’ I ask, referring to the Chicago organised crime bosses, both of whom had powerful connections including to the CIA and who were both murdered in mob hits a few years later.

‘Don't overblow the mafia thing; I was never in bed with those guys,’ he flashes, a hint of irritation in his voice. ‘Frankie ran with the mafia, yes that’s true, everyone knew that. It was an Italian thing with him – ties to the old country meant no distinction between right and wrong for him. You were either Italian or you weren't, and if you were, then the mafia was as much a part of your identity as Pizza and the Pope. To me, they were there, but always in the shadows, in the background and I was careful to keep my distance. You know, I even split from Frankie when I became President to put more distance between me and them, even though I loved that guy like a brother,' Kennedy states defensively, shifting in his chair.

'Fine but didn't Giancana and Hoffa deliver you Chicago in the election in return for a promise of going easy on organised crime?' I challenge him, bringing in "The Hoff" – Jimmy Hoffa – to the conversation. Hoffa, convicted criminal and controversial leader of the Teamsters union, was reputedly in bed with the two mafia bosses, and coincidentally was also murdered by the mob some years later.

'Hm, hardly. Chicago was delivered by Mayor Daley and the Democratic party machine, plain and simple. And besides, if the Mob delivered anything other than a hot pizza in Chicago, then that was without my connivance,' he states aggressively. 'And they certainly backed the wrong horse, didn't they, what with Bobby's crackdown on organised crime and the Teamsters,' he adds for good measure.

But despite his assertions, the mafia connections are too strong to be brushed away. There are simply too many coincidences to let the topic slide, and it's important from a national security standpoint as well: the confluence of geopolitics and dirty money, potentially forging convenient alliances between organised crime and the political establishment of the day. I need to see where this one goes.

'La Bahía de Cochinos – The Bay of Pigs,' I pause for effect. 'Were the Mafia the driving force behind the invasion?' I ask, referring to the covert operation to invade Cuba and unseat Fidel Castro that ended in farce.

'American foreign policy was the driving force behind the special military operation. Castro had to go,' Kennedy retorts curtly.

'Yes, but the Mob lost a ton under Castro. Lansky, Trafficante, and the bosses dropped millions as he turned the tables on them. It was personal for them. They developed a visceral hatred for Castro after he kicked them out of the country,' I state, referring to Castro's expulsion of the American mafia after the 1959 Cuban revolution. 'They wanted him dead. They wanted their casinos and hotels back. They had cause...and the means.'

'The Mob came later. The Bay of Pigs was entirely a CIA led operation, initiated under Eisenhower and sanctioned by me. A communist presence on our doorstep was intolerable. It allowed Khrushchev to hold a knife to America's throat – it gave the Soviets a base in the Western hemisphere. Castro knew that and knew how to play the Soviets against us. But it didn't stop there. Cuba was a tumour sitting right off the coast, ready to metastasis and spread communism across the Americas, just as the Spanish had used it as a beachhead to conquer South America. No US President could stand idly by. As I said, Castro had to go,' he states firmly.

'Then why go in with a half-baked operation consisting of mercenaries and other irregulars that had little chance of success?' I ask, given the operation was a monumental cockup from start to finish.

'You say "little chance of success" but that was not the intelligence we had at that time. Castro was dragging the country into poverty, tearing up its social fabric and alienating large swathes of the population, including significant vested interests. The place was ripe for counter revolution. We were in contact with many disaffected elements who were just waiting for the right conditions to overthrow Castro and swing in behind us. The strategy was correct, but, yes, I admit the tactics were off, and I'll take that one on the chin.'

'But if your Intelligence was so good, why were the Cubans waiting for you on the beach, at the Playa Girón?'

Kennedy regards me with a hint of distrust in his eyes, contemplating his response. I prod him: 'So, why was your invasion wrapped up by the Cuban counter offensive in just three days, barely making it off the beach?'

He purses his lips. 'We had a mole.'

'A mole?'

'Yup, a mole. Johnny Havana.'

'Johnny Havana? That's not a name I've heard of before,' I say, scratching my cheek.

'Good ole Johnny Havana,' he sighs, sarcastically. 'When the whole thing unravelled the spooks went on a witch hunt, trying to find out how they got it so wrong. They couldn't believe they'd cocked it up so badly. They had some serious egg on their face. So, they came up with Johnny Havana, a diehard anti-communist exile in the Miami Cuban community, who was involved in raising and training Brigade 2506, the special operation's force. Johnny, however, happened to be playing both sides of the Florida Straits; he was also in Castro's pocket and leaked the US operational plans weeks in advance.'

'So, *who* was Johnny?' I ask.

'It was a code name for the mole, not a real name, something the spooks came up with. Johnny could have been anyone of up to five people – the whole operation leaked like a sieve – but no one ever cracked under interrogation. Maybe Johnny didn't even exist. Maybe he was just an excuse to divert blame. Maybe he was just a metaphor for how not to run a covert operation.' Kennedy shrugs.

'We can agree then that the whole thing was poorly conceived and even more poorly executed. But, I wonder, was it Johnny Havana or John F. Kennedy, who ultimately doomed the invasion to failure?'

Kennedy looks at me, narrowing his eyes, his forehead creased.

I press on. 'It was you and you alone who made the last-minute decision to pull the air cover, leaving the invasion force badly exposed.'

He stares at me, remaining silent, eyes cold.

'Let me quote Pepe San Román then, the Brigade commander on the ground: "The Americans lost their nerve and left us for dead." And according to him, despite the Cubans expecting them, they could have still pushed on if they'd had the air cover, but without it was game over. So, Mr President,' I continue in an accusatory tone, 'why *did you* pull that air cover?'

Kennedy exhales and looks away, before coming back to meet my gaze. 'It was complicated. Special military operations are always complicated,' he replies, in a guarded tone. I notice he's persistently used the innocuous term "special military operation," carefully avoiding the word "invasion."

'*Complicated*?' I echo, sensing he's dissembling.

'Yeah.' He shifts in his chair. 'There were a lot of moving parts, you know, a lot of communications back and forth between the Agency, the military, the White House, that kind of stuff. Wires got crossed. I mean, frankly speaking, coordination was not the best and well...the landings got ahead of the planned air sorties, and it was kind of too late to send the planes in, the game was up and US involvement would have been, erm, too obvious,' he replies, with a sheepish look.

'So, to avoid *complications* Brigade 2506 were abandoned to their fate?' I question, with a strong hint of disapproval – although I shouldn't be surprised at the political cynicism of it all.

It's called "Realpolitik" and it was round one of a long game. Soldiers know the risk,' he replies defensively.

'And I presume round two was the Mob, recruiting Giancana and Roselli to bump off Castro in return for getting their casinos back in Havana? A classic Adam and Eve operation to keep the Administration's nose clean,' I press, referring to the improbably named Operation Roulette, the attempt twelve months later by the CIA, enlisting the Mob, to achieve what had failed so spectacularly at the Bay of Pigs.

'"Adam and Eve?"' Kennedy quizzes.

'Yeah, Adam and Eve, creating a fig leaf to conceal the identities of the people really calling the shots, thereby creating plausible deniability. In the Agency's own words, and I quote: "a sensitive operation requiring support of non-state actors who operate outside of normal judicial frameworks." It's all there in the files,' I state, holding up my notes.

'Or *implausible* deniability,' he snorts. 'If you really want to know the truth, it was more "Get Smart" than "007," a comedy of errors: exploding cigars, poisoned pills, booby trapped cars, midnight fast boat runs across the Straits. To be honest, Castro's network of double agents and sympathizers in Florida was better than ours in Cuba and that probably saved him. Nothing came of Operation Roulette except more red faces at the Agency.' He shrugs resignedly.

'Except the Mob got something out of it, didn't they? A free reign to build their new Jerusalem in Las Vegas, while the Agency kept the Feds off their back as a quid pro quo for turning Cold War warriors in Cuba,' I hasten to add, not wanting to let slide the fact that the Mafia got a generous pay off despite the failure of the comical operation.

'Some compromises were odious,' he agrees. 'But that was more Bobby's department than mine.' There we go again, passing the ball to Bobby on law and order, I note to myself.

'Which then brings us back to Judith, doesn't it? She would have been dating Giancana at about the same time as Operation Roulette, right?' Kennedy looks sideways, bored. 'Given you were still *friendly* with Judith, she could've been a useful conduit between the White House and the Mob's anti-Castro operations, right?'

'The Washington Post and Church Committee archives are all online, you can draw your own conclusions,' he replies, with a hint of annoyance. 'And besides, I told you, Justice was Bobby's department.'

I smile to myself at that comment. 'I've read them,' I say, 'cover to cover and the obvious conclusion is that there is *no* conclusion.'

'Again, I can categorically tell you, I did not have relationships with the Mob. There's nothing more to say on the matter, period,' Kennedy states firmly and with finality, squaring up in his chair, folding his arms across his chest.

Okay, well fair enough, I think to myself. The records are inconclusive, and no prosecutor would attempt a case on the available evidence, which while abundant is still largely circumstantial. I glance at my watch.

'And one more thing mister,' Kennedy leans forward, piercing me with his gaze, as he points a finger towards me. 'When all's said and done, despite all the bungling and the obvious moral comprises, this whole get-Castro-thing was no jingoistic anti-communist crusade, no patriotic show for the voters, nor simple muscle flexing to keep the right-wing establishment at bay. No, this was actually about dealing with a threat to the very existence of the United States,' he states with conviction. 'You know about the U-2 photos, right?'

'You mean the ones taken in October '62 by the U-2 spy plane over Cuba?' I ask, wanting to make sure he's alluding to the photos that precipitated the Cuban missile crisis, that brought the world to the brink of atomic war.

'You got that right. Well, those photos clearly showed construction of a Soviet SS-4 launch facility in San Cristóbal. Within a matter of months, maybe even weeks, the Soviets would have had both medium and intermediate range ballistic missiles ninety miles off the coast of Florida, pointing straight down our throats, completely changing the strategic calculus in the Western hemisphere. Gives meaning to the anti-Castro efforts, huh?'

I give a non-committal nod in reply.

'The top Brass and the Agency were straining at the leash. This was their big chance to give the Commies a bloody nose and get their revenge for the Bay of Pigs. Everyone was banging the war drums, baying for blood, so much so that people lost clarity and judgement. The Joint Chiefs of Staff and most of the National Security Council all agreed that a full-scale invasion of Cuba was the only way to get rid of those launch sites. But I had serious concerns, as did McNamara, that this would lead to open military confrontation with the Soviets and likely trigger an atomic war that neither side could win. In the end, I overrode them, and we went with a naval blockade to stop the Soviets delivering any more missiles and materiel into Cuba.'

He leans back in his chair, his affability returning. 'Most people knew, or at least think they knew, that the world was on the edge of an atomic war in '62, but nothing could have been further from the truth – not once we put the blockade in place.' He smiles, a little smugly.

'That's news to me. That's certainly not the way it looked from the living rooms of middle America, I can assure you!' I retort, recalling the collective white-knuckle anxiety that gripped a nation – and indeed the world – as we watched the missile crisis unfold on our television sets.

'And that's the way we needed it to look,' Kennedy continues. 'No one could know what was really going on behind the scenes. Khrushchev had his redlines, we knew that and turning back Soviet cargo ships in the middle of the Caribbean Sea was not one of them – at least that's what I was prepared to take a calculated gamble on.'

'That's one hell of a gamble, isn't it? I mean, risking World War Three?' I state, running my fingers through my hair.

'Was it?' He raises his eyebrows. 'I'd met Khrushchev; I'd met others in the Politburo. I'd formed a judgment pretty quickly that their poker game relied on bluff. They didn't know what cards we held, but they knew their hand wasn't strong if it came to an atomic exchange and they guessed correctly that they were heavily outnumbered on a warhead basis. After Khrushchev's initial public bluster about breaking the blockade and threatening war, I raised the stakes, moving to DEFCON 2, putting a hundred and eighty bombers on continuous airborne alert, including twenty-three B-52's always within strike range of Soviet soil. I was in effect calling their bluff.' He smiles again, leaning back, locking his hands behind his head, looking very satisfied with himself.

'Nonetheless, the room for error and miscalculation was surely still immense, was it not, making it a very risky play?' I ask, debating in my mind whether this man was a master tactician with uncanny nerves of steel, or had a massive streak of beginner's luck on his side.

'I guess there was a wild card in the pack, yes, a card that could have screwed everything up,' Kennedy replies, looking contemplative but nonetheless unconcerned.

'And that was what?' I ask.

'And that was Castro. He didn't really believe in all that international brotherhood of the workers BS, that was all for show. There was only one thing he believed in and that was Fidel Castro. As much as the Soviets thought he was their puppet, Castro thought *he* was the puppet master playing the global powers. We could control the play with Khrushchev, but not with Castro. He could easily have pulled us all into a war by making a rash move that we – or the Soviets – would have had no choice but to respond to. He nearly goddam did it as well, by opening fire on one of our spy planes, which the boys in the Pentagon wanted to treat as a de facto act of war by the Soviets!'

He chuckles, again showing no signs of concern, unlike me.

'So, you got lucky with that one, right? And in fact, you also got lucky a second time, didn't you?'

'A second time?' Kennedy raises his eyebrows.

'Yes. When Vasili Arkhipov – "the man who saved the world" – had the courage and good sense not to sanction an atomic launch against the US,' I state.

'Oh yeah?' Kennedy queries, arching his eyebrows.

'Oh yes. You know who I'm talking about. The Executive Officer onboard Russian submarine B-59, that was patrolling off the Cuban coast. The boat that came under depth charge attack by the US navy. It was Arkhipov that refused to allow the boat's captain, Valentin Savitsky, to launch an atomic strike, when he believed – not unfairly – that Russia was already at war with the US, having lost radio communications with Moscow several days earlier.'

I look at my notes, made from files declassified in 2022 by the Russian Defence Ministry and quote Arkhipov's now famous words to Savitsky: '"Comrade Captain, if we are not at war with the United States, then once you press that button we will be;

and if we are already at war, then any actions taken by this boat are inconsequential. The choice is clear; is your conscience?"'

I look up at Kennedy, to check his reaction.

He smiles cynically. 'Well, thank God there's always a cool head in a crisis, even in the Russian navy,' he responds dismissively, displaying an almost cavalier disregard for how close his play with Khrushchev came to unravelling and triggering an all-out thermonuclear war. 'Look,' he continues, leaning forward, 'there's always the potential for mishaps and accidents, but at the end of the day, the Soviets backed down and turned their ships around. Crisis averted. Did we get lucky? Maybe. But what we did get was a victory: Soviet missiles out of the Western hemisphere and egg on Khrushchev's face. Who dares wins, right?' he states with a smug smile. 'And besides,' he continues, 'we now had the psychological advantage, the upper hand for future conflicts. The Soviets knew we were serious and would go to the wire.'

'It would be fair to say that conflict was a hallmark of your presidency, wouldn't it?' I add.

'The times we lived in – the Cold War,' he replies philosophically.

'Cuba, Laos, Vietnam, West Berlin – Berlin multiple times, in fact. You and Khrushchev, equals and opposites, playing a game of cat and mouse, stalking each other around the chess board,' I continue. 'But maybe there was no greater symbol of the cold war than Berlin, no demarcation line between you and Khrushchev that held more potential for the Cold War turning hot,' I state.

'True.' Kennedy stretches his jaw and rubs his chin. 'West Berlin was a perennial millstone, certainly for Khrushchev at any rate. A Western bastion, untouchable, planted in their backyard, taunting them daily. Khrushchev was determined to change that. He'd made it his personal mission to remove us from West Berlin. He'd given a commitment to the Red Army Generals, who were still smarting from the fact that they'd liberated Berlin at the cost of so much Russian blood but after the war the Yalta agreement allowed the Allies to march in and take control of the Western sector. As you know, the Soviet's first attempt to kick us out by imposing a total land blockade in '49 failed, thanks to the Allies' airbridge into Tempelhof airport. Khrushchev scoffed at Stalin behind his back for allowing this failure, but he ultimately paid the price for that piece of schadenfreude years later, during the crisis of '61 in fact.'

'You're referring to the Check Point Charlie incident, I assume, in October of that year?'

'Right. Khrushchev was bringing things to a head, crossing lines, interfering with our free movement into the eastern sector of Berlin, which was guaranteed by treaty. There were a number of clashes – though nothing hot at that stage – across the demarcation line that divided East from West, and they were growing daily. It was getting tense and had the potential to blow up. Khrushchev was testing our resolve, my resolve, in fact. We knew through intercepted cables he really believed he could win this one, stare us down. There was even one cable,' he chuckles, amused, 'where Khrushchev referred to me as "the playboy who'll piss his pants as soon as he thinks he's staring down the barrel of atomic annihilation – West Berlin is as good as ours."'

'Hence, this became a personal pissing match between you and Khrushchev?' I challenge him.

He ignores my comment and continues. 'In response, we sent a cable of our own, to the U.S. Embassy in Moscow, warning them to prepare for a possible atomic first strike against Russian military installations, in the event the Soviets deployed overwhelming conventional land forces against us in Berlin. Now of course, the cable was intended to be *intercepted* by the Soviets – to which they duly obliged – to put them on the back foot and force a change in their strategic calculus. We followed up with further cables giving details of airfields and bases that would supposedly be attacked, to lend further credibility to the play.'

'And were you just bluffing? Or did you actually consider launching a first strike if Khrushchev overstepped the mark in Berlin?' I ask while images from the Cold War movie "Dr.

Strangelove or: How I Learned to Stop Worrying and Love the Bomb" flash through my mind. In particular, I'm picturing the scene where Major T.J. "King" Kong is riding an atomic bomb like a rodeo cowboy, heading straight for atomic destruction.

Kennedy chuckles disarmingly. 'I told you before, it's a poker game. There's no need to go to war, if you're prepared to go to war. It's a question of will and resolve – is yours greater than that of your enemy's?'

'Hmm, I see, so when the American tank platoon squared off against the Soviets at Checkpoint Charlie, both sides armed with live rounds, and the entire world holding its breath for a nerve-wracking twenty-four hours – while contemplating the brink of atomic annihilation – you were certain of the outcome?' I ask, questioning his sangfroid – or perhaps his sanity.

'Nothing's ever certain, you can never predict one hundred percent how the cards are gonna fall,' he chuckles, 'but the tanks pulled back, and the Soviets retreated behind their wall, for good. Therefore, a win to us.'

'Okay, but wasn't the construction of the Berlin Wall a defeat in its own right? Not just a breach of post war treaties but a monumental blow to the hopes of all people living under Soviet occupation? A riposte to the American clarion call for freedom and self-determination?' I challenge him, wondering if Checkpoint Charlie was a pyrrhic victory for Kennedy and a real win for Khrushchev.

Kennedy sets his jaw and leans forward. 'You've got to remember Khrushchev's goal was to unify Berlin under Soviet control. He already had East Berlin, so what did building a wall give him other than signalling a retreat behind his own lines, only to peer over the parapets impotently at his enemies?' Kennedy counters.

'So round one to you, I guess and also round two after the Cuban missile crisis, which happened hot on the heels of Berlin.' I pause for a moment, mulling something. 'So, was it getting personal between you and Khrushchev? I mean, you were lurching from one crisis to the next, with him on the other side, right?

Was there a personal battle of egos playing out here?'

'No,' he replies firmly. 'You can't allow egos or emotions to play a part in these things, especially when the fate of humanity hangs in the balance. I didn't bear any ill will towards Khrushchev – other than the fact that he was a commie.' He smiles. 'To me the struggle was bigger than any single man. It was a battle of ideals, a contest between civilizations, between tyranny and freedom, good and evil,' he states with evident self-belief.

'I see. You mentioned earlier that Khrushchev had staked his credibility with the Party on gaining West Berlin. I imagine your famous visit there in '63 was the final straw that broke the camel's back, in terms of his credibility and hastened his political demise – *despite* there being nothing personal between you,' I suggest, raising my eyebrows.

'Despite our success in pushing the Soviets back in October '61, Berlin was still an open-ended issue, and in fact, it was an issue that wouldn't be resolved for another generation. No American president could stand by and allow Soviet interference in Berlin. It was a totemic issue for us that symbolized everything the Cold War was about. My visit in '63 was designed to make that point to the Soviets, in no uncertain terms, much to the chagrin of Khrushchev, who still clung to the hope of gaining control over the Western sector.'

'Is it true McGeorge Bundy, your National Security Advisor, stated to you at the time of your visit to Berlin, that: "this'll be the death knell for Khrushchev. He'll be lucky if they don't shuffle him off to some god-awful re-education camp in Siberia,"' I quote, glancing at my notes.

'Something like that,' Kennedy replies.

'Your Berlin speech of course etched those immortal words "Ich bin ein Berliner" in the minds of a generation and indeed for generations to come – where did your inspiration for those lines come from?' I ask.

'Oh, you know, I had good speech writers,' he replies modestly. 'But you know what? I think we were just imitating the Romans,' he adds.

'The Romans?' I echo, surprised.

'"Civis Romanus sum,"' he quotes in response.

'"I am a citizen of Rome?"' I guess.

'Correct. Two thousand years ago there was no prouder proclamation than to declare oneself a citizen of Rome. Hence the borrowed pride and defiance in my proclamation: "I am a Berliner."'

'And of course, amplified by that lesser-known, but more potent challenge to the Soviets: "Lasst sie nach Berlin kommen," – "Let them come to Berlin,"' I add for good measure.

'Indeed. Khrushchev reportedly winced when he heard that one and mumbled, or so the story goes, that he might as well load the gun and put it to his own head before the KGB came for him.'

'And fast forward thirty years, the implacable opposition to any Soviet interference in West Berlin that you embedded in American foreign policy, culminated in the ultimate victory when the Wall came down in November '91, right?'

He shifts in his seat, looking a little reticent. 'There were many hammers that chipped away at that wall over the intervening decades. I can hardly take credit for it all. In fact, the credit should go to Reagan.'

'Although Reagan saw it slightly differently, reputedly saying at the time: "this is Jack's victory. Jack laid the foundations that led to this momentous day, this blow for freedom, the death knell of the Soviet Empire,"' I quote, to which Kennedy simply dips his head in acknowledgement.

Conscious of the time, I return to my notes, thumbing through them. 'Did your experiences as a soldier during the Second World War play a role in how you managed high stakes situations, such as Berlin? I mean in terms of how you faced conflict?' I ask, pivoting to an earlier and formative chapter in Kennedy's life.

'I only played a small part in that war, a very small part. There were many others who did far more than me,' he replies modestly.

'A part nonetheless typified by tenacity and courage, that must have played a part in shaping your later struggle against Communism?' I add.

Kennedy stays silent, a contemplative look in his eyes, as he stares at the wall behind me. 'I could have done more, much more, maybe even made the ultimate sacrifice like Joe Jr…' he states ruefully, sounding a little emotional as memories of Joe Jr, his beloved brother who died on a special combat mission over the English Channel, come flooding back.

My bad.

'You did your part, and you can hold your head high. You were right in the thick of it,' I say, setting the record straight. 'Unlike some of your successors who chose to stay home when it was their turn to serve their country,' I add pointedly.

Kennedy just looks at me though, with a faint, tired smile, before pulling himself back to the present.

'You were something of a gambler though, weren't you? Like when you took on that Japanese destroyer in the Solomon Islands, with your PT boat, which was really nothing more than a motor launch with a couple of torpedo tubes strapped to the sides.'

Kennedy shakes his head, smiling to himself. 'It was a dark moonless night. I can assure you if I'd known I was attacking a destroyer I would have turned tail and headed the other way – at full speed!'

'Unfortunately for you and your crew, the "Amagiri" rammed PT-109, literally cutting it in half leaving you for dead, right?'

'Yup, cut clean in half and there we were left clinging to the wreckage in the dark.'

'Swim or surrender, I presume?'

'Ah hah. I gave the men the choice to swim or surrender, yes. Surrender was probably the better option, given we were drifting in a strong current, clinging to wreckage, and trying to keep several severely burnt men alive.'

'Hence, you swam for it I assume?'

He nods his head. 'We swam all night, trying to avoid Japanese search parties. At sunrise, we spotted an island about three and a half miles southwest of our position and struck out for it. It was a tough swim though. The current was heading due north, causing us to drift off course and I was towing an injured man by a rope.'

'By your teeth by all accounts,' I add.

'Yeah, that one cost me a lot of dental work later,' he says with a wry smile. 'But that wasn't the worst of it. When we were within half a mile of the shoreline, one of the men spotted fins in the water – about a dozen of them, swarming in a kinda frenzy. Definitely not something you want to swim towards. We debated whether to let the current take us back out to sea and then go around them, but we agreed we'd probably lack the energy to swim back in against the current, to reach the other side of the island.'

'So, what did you do?' I ask, just the thought of being stranded in the water surrounded by sharks being enough to put me on edge.

'We just kept heading towards those fins, which I can tell you, was a damn sight more daunting than facing down a Japanese destroyer! When we got to the edge of the shark pack, they started to show an interest in us, a few of them nudging and bumping us, testing us I guess.'

'Every sailor's nightmare,' I say, imagining the terror of being surrounded by a shiver of sharks – probably Oceanic whitetips – with nothing more than then the wreckage of PT 109 for protection.

'The Ensign and Gunner's Mate had the idea of lunging at them with some broken spars, and I fired a flare gun into one of them. That seemed to dampen their enthusiasm for a while and then you've never seen ten men swim as fast as we did.' He grins, no doubt recalling the relief of making it to the shore with limbs intact, a few of the men suffering nothing more than lacerations from the encounter. 'But unfortunately, our troubles didn't end there, in fact they just began. There was no water or food on the island – Plum Pudding island it was called, ironically. A few days later we were forced to swim again to a neighbouring island, Olsana, about four miles southeast of Plum Pudding. Getting back in the water nearly caused a mutiny though.'

He smiles. 'But it was either swim with the sharks or die of thirst. Nonetheless, I think that was the longest swim of our lives. But once we got to Olsana, we soon discovered there was no water there either and by now the crew were in pretty bad shape. Most of them were suffering from severe dehydration and the injuries sustained in the attack on the "Amagiri."'

'A grim situation indeed.'

'Yeah, we basically had one last chance. We spotted another island about six miles south of Olsana. Ensign Ross and I set out that night and reached the shore just before dawn. We made our way inland but were surprised by a Japanese patrol. My weapon jammed, probably due to overexposure to the saltwater, as I tried to engage a soldier who almost stumbled into me in the semi-darkness. Luckily, they hadn't seen Ross, who opened fire and dropped the man in front of me, giving me time to clear my jam. In the ensuing firefight, we overwhelmed the Japanese and took some prisoners – they were in a pretty poor state themselves, actually. More importantly, we found canned provisions and a fifty-gallon drum of drinking water, which I canoed back to the men on Olsana. We were rescued a few days later after native coast watchers discovered us and reported our location to allied forces.'

'That's quite the war story,' I state, impressed at his courage and determination in the face of such daunting odds. 'Did you ever think you wouldn't, erm, make it?' I ask cautiously.

'I think the only time I genuinely despaired was when we made it to Olsana and found nothing to drink, other than rainwater. But I'm a born optimist and I think that optimism kept me going. I firmly believed we'd eventually get rescued, as long as we kept taking control of the situation and refused to give up,' Kennedy replies. 'But you know what, if it wasn't for Gasa and Kumana, it could have been a very different outcome.'

'Gasa and Kumana? The native coastwatchers?'

'Yup. If they hadn't been scouting the islands on the off chance of finding survivors from PT-109, we could have all perished,' he states solemnly.

'You even invited them to your inauguration in Washington, didn't you?'

'Sure did. Shame they never made it,' he states wistfully.

'You might be interested to know, I visited Kumana in Honiara in 2007. He remembered you, of course, even had a tear in his eye when he told me the story of your rescue. Unfortunately, Gasa passed away some years earlier of lung cancer. But his son still tells the tale of how his father nearly emptied his Tommy gun into you in fright, when he was confronted by this bearded and bedraggled sunburnt devil, emerging semi naked from the bush.' Kennedy smiles gently, pursing his lip and looks away from me.

'So, let me ask you, did your first-hand experience of war influence you in any way as a politician, as President of the United States?' I ask, curious about how personal experiences of war affects politicians once they're in high office. Are they more inclined to make peace or make war? Or in Kennedy's case, make love.

He pauses before responding, a grave mood settling over him. 'Once you've experienced war, avoiding it becomes all the more imperative. But that shouldn't be confused with the need to confront potential enemies head-on and engage in deterrence through force, if necessary. Appeasement is not a strategy for achieving peace. We learnt that in the 1930s.'

'So how about the Peace Corps? Did you establish that based on your war time experience?'

'Yes, in part but it was also a response to the steady stream of young volunteers from Communist countries willing to spread their cause across the globe under the guise of social and charitable work. If they could do it, why shouldn't we be encouraging the flower of American youth to spend time in the field in developing countries, carrying out public good and showing the best of America to the world?' he responds with conviction.

'Therefore in a sense the Peace Corps was another front in the Cold War, albeit a projection of soft, not hard power?'

'In some ways, yes,' Kennedy confirms, candidly.

'And your race to space, was that also in response to the Soviets? I mean when they put Yuri Gagarin into space in '61. I imagine that must have been a real jolt to national pride.'

'More than a jolt to pride,' he snorts. 'It put the Soviets on a trajectory that had implications for military supremacy across a range of capabilities such as satellites, missiles, jet engines and so on. This was a race we didn't want to lose, although there were many doubters in Congress who saw it as a waste of money and effort.'

'Including yourself prior to the Gagarin shock, I should add.'

'Hmm. The investment case suddenly looked a whole lot more appealing.' He pauses and then adds enigmatically: 'And not just because of the Soviets.'

My ears prick up at that last comment. 'What do you mean by that: "not just because of the Soviets?"'

'You wouldn't believe me if I told you,' Kennedy replies dismissively, which of course only piques my curiosity further.

'Try me,' I insist, edging forward.

'There was something else up there, not just the Soviets... maybe, possibly.' Kennedy sounds unsure of himself but continues, nonetheless. 'There were sightings, encounters, *certain* incidents.'

'What do you mean by that? What kind of encounters?' I ask, unsure of where he's going with this.

'We knew the Soviets were ahead of us in space, after the Gagarin thing but not *that* far ahead. Not to the point where their spacecraft could leave and re-enter the atmosphere at will and buzz our planes. The evidence was never conclusive, certainly not in my opinion but also not so inconclusive that it could be ignored either. I mean, I'm a level-headed guy but how do you explain a spacecraft that travels at speeds above Mach

10 and then comes to a sudden halt, just like that and then just hovers in the air. Soviets? Maybe, but highly unlikely. Chinese? No way, not back then. So then what?' His forehead creases and he sounds genuinely puzzled.

'UFO's?' I venture, half in jest.

Kennedy remains serious. 'It's a possibility we couldn't entirely dismiss. There were too many unexplained phenomena. They were never released but U-2 pilots such as Powers took some pretty clear photos and provided credible first-hand accounts of being buzzed on several missions, along with other evidence from military and civilian sources,' he responds soberly.

'Coincidentally, the Pentagon just released three videos of so-called unidentified flying phenomena captured on camera by navy pilots, the encounters not being dissimilar to what you've just described,' I inform him.

'I'm not surprised,' he replies, without a hint of shock.

'I wonder if Apollo 11 found *anything* on the moon? I mean, anything that's still classified to this day?' I ask cautiously, wondering if the Kennedy administration's mission to the moon had a hidden purpose shielded from public view.

Kennedy arches his eyebrows and gives me a puzzled look. 'Maybe, but the Apollo moon landing was six years after my time.'

Yeah of course. I suck in air through my teeth. My bad – he was dead by then.

'Was it all worth it though? The expense, the diversion of resources and national focus that could have gone into other programs back home that would have made a material difference to peoples' lives, to the social and political agenda of the day?'

'It's the wrong question. You can't measure nation building initiatives in terms of dollars and cents. Space was there, so it had to be explored, Soviets or no Soviets. Mankind abhors a vacuum. We have an insatiable thirst to understand and gain control of our surroundings. It's almost a god-like complex, a need to master the elements, whether terrestrial or beyond. That's how we progress as a species, by continually pushing the boundaries, expanding outwards, sometimes with negative results but always with inevitability. The space program represented the zeitgeist of the times in that sense, just as Columbus and the European discovery of the Americas did five hundred years earlier,' he exclaims with genuine passion.

'"We choose to go to the Moon."' I echo his famous words that set the tone for the American race to space some sixty years earlier.

Kennedy smiles in response, before continuing to extol his point. 'The irony is that history has taught us little. We've forgotten the lesson of the "Gagarin shock" and the nation building aspirations it triggered, we've allowed ourselves to slip back into complacency.

He leans forward, eyes steady and voice measured, touched with a solemn look. 'You remember my inaugural line, yes? "Ask not what your country can do for you – ask what you can do for your country." Those words weren't just platitudes; they captured a fundamental truth about nationhood – about the covenant between a people and their shared destiny.'

He pauses, as if weighing the weight of the decades. 'A nation is more than just geography or government. It's a call to collective responsibility and sacrifice, a shared idea that binds disparate individuals into something greater than themselves.'

'But today,' he continues, his gaze sharpening, 'I see that idea under threat, not from foreign armies – or not just from foreign armies - but from voices that pit citizen against citizen, that stoke fears instead of hope.'

He lets out a slow breath. 'Populists are on the rise, climbing on the back of real grievances but exploiting them by channelling resentment toward "the other": immigrants, foreigners, those who seem different, even fellow citizens who are all too easily labelled as the "class enemy." They tap into deep, atavistic instincts – worry about safety, identity, belonging – that simply don't die out in our DNA.'

I nod, sensing the gravity, then press further. 'But isn't some of that backlash also the fault of so-called conventional politicians, like yourself? Those who have allowed mass immigration without effective integration, failed to manage soaring housing costs, encouraged the offshoring of large swathes of the economy and let inequality deepen? Aren't these real hardships that create fertile ground for populists to exploit?'

Kennedy nods in agreement. "Of course. Neglect and mismanagement leave people feeling abandoned and unheard. When basic needs like jobs and housing or community cohesion are neglected, fear and resentment take root. Populists excel at channelling that frustration into divisive rhetoric.'

He leans back slightly, the reverence returning. 'True nation-building requires the opposite – a profound commitment to unity and the nation, a willingness to set aside narrow interests for the common good. It's about lifting each other, about recognizing the contribution of every individual to the larger whole, regardless of their origin or political stripes.'

'I fear,' he says candidly, 'that without a renewal of that spirit, trust in our institutions will continue to degrade. Our democracy depends not just on laws and courts, but on a shared belief in the nation's ideals and their daily practice.'

'And then,' Kennedy's voice takes on a note both urgent and reflective, 'you add the power of technology – artificial intelligence, mass data, and the algorithms shaping what millions see and believe. These tools can enlighten or they can mislead; they can empower or enslave. Without wisdom and a higher purpose guiding their use, we risk surrendering the very agency that defines free societies.'

He fixes me with a pointed look. 'The challenge is clear: to reclaim the meaning of citizenship, to resist the siren calls that divide us, and to harness the unprecedented power of technology in service of truth and nationhood – not division and distrust.' He pauses as if looking to an unseen horizon. 'History reminds us that nations rise and fall on the strength of their unity and purpose. The great question facing us now is whether we have the resolve to face this moment, to act with courage and conviction, and to ask not just what the nation can do for each of us, but what each of us must do for the nation – together.'

He nods firmly at me, the weight of his conviction filling the room. 'If we fail that test, not one threat from abroad will be so damaging as the death of the American idea from within.'

'It sounds like you may want to have a conversation with the current incumbent in the White House,' I state, half-jokingly.

He rolls his eyes and snorts. 'I'm just an echo from the past – who's going to listen to me?'

'Although, maybe we need lessons from the past right now,' I reply, smiling.

'No doubt, but no one takes history lessons from ghosts anymore,' he replies resignedly.

I glance at my watch. His spectral lament, as it happens, serves as the perfect segue to the final topic I want to discuss, saving the best to last. You see, there's a part of the Kennedy story that still haunts us to this day, refusing to rest in peace – echoes from a traumatic event that shook the world sixty years ago. It's an event so steeped in controversy and mystery, riddled with inconsistencies, coincidences, and improbabilities that perhaps only one man can fully solve it and that's the man sitting in front of me!

I clear my throat, shifting in my chair, preparing to fire the bazooka. Kennedy twitches in response; he senses something big is coming. Here goes:

'Mr. President...*who* assassinated you?'

Kennedy's eyes widen in surprise as he recoils, the bluntness of my question catching him off guard. An uncomfortable silence immediately envelops the room. He takes his time to respond, slowly meeting my gaze, fixing me with a cold stare. 'Lee. Harvey. Oswald,' he replies, slowly and deliberately, his voice icy and resolute.

'Lee Harvey Oswald? A lone gunman? Just one disgruntled Marine holed up in a book depository, able to think, plan, and execute a plot to assassinate the President of the United States... come on, really?' I say with incredulity.

Kennedy remains emotionless, regarding me.

'It just doesn't stack up. It makes no sense. There are too many coincidences, too many loose ends to simply dismiss this as the work of a single assassin,' I continue vehemently.

He exhales heavily. 'Look, those old coals have been raked over so many times: the Warren Commission; the House Select Committee on Assassinations; the Rockefeller Commission, all pointing to the same conclusion. What do people want? An endless parade of official enquiries until they finally get an answer that suits their conspiracy theories? It's not going to happen. Let it rest. Accept the fact that the obvious answer *is* the answer.'

'That's as maybe, but all of those Commissions have a whiff of incompleteness about them, an almost deliberate lack of enthusiasm to dig deep and chase the evidence to ground, as if they didn't want to rock the boat, preferring a convenient untruth. Besides, if you listen to the private conversations of Washington insiders in their moments of candour, you hear a very different story. Take LBJ's views for instance, and I quote "the more I hear and learn about the events surrounding that fateful day, the more I doubt that Oswald could have single handedly prosecuted such a momentous plot. Something doesn't add up here." Or even many decades later another Democrat President, according to Monica Lewinsky, told her: "if I revealed what I now know about the Kennedy assassination, it would shake the American peoples' belief in our system of government and its institutions – some truths are better left alone." But for me, I can ignore as outlandish coincidences the Zapruder film; the grassy knoll; "badge man;" the apparent ineptitude of multiple law enforcement agencies; and so on.

'However, there is one event I cannot ignore and simply put down to coincidence, and that's Jack Ruby's so-called assassination of Lee Harvey Oswald in the basement of the Dallas police headquarters. How can you or anyone explain that away as just some freak event?' I continue, pushing hard, still not able to fathom after all these years why Ruby, a total stranger, would walk into a Dallas police station and casually gun down Oswald in broad daylight, in front of the nation's assembled press.

Kennedy looks pensive, clenching his fists and straightening them out again. 'Hmm. Jack Ruby was the joker in the pack,' he states, his voice tinged with a mix of bitterness and regret, as he turns his gaze away from me.

My ears prick up at this. '"Joker in the pack?" What do you mean by that?' I ask, leaning in.

'Take Clinton's advice, let it be,' he replies irritated.

Nope, we're going to keep going, I say to myself. 'I want to know what you meant by that,' I persist.

'Forget it fella, it means nothing,' he replies, as if regretting his words.

'No, you meant something. Come on, *why* was Ruby the "joker in the pack?"' I persist.

Kennedy pauses, chewing his bottom lip, clearly debating something in his mind. He lets out a deep sigh. 'If I tell you, they'll kill you,' he states with what I assume is mock gravity.

'Okay, I'll take the secret to the grave then,' I respond lightly, smiling.

Kennedy's face tightens with a mix of reluctance and concern. 'Are you sure? This is deadly serious. Are you *really* sure you want to know?'

'Yes,' I reply emphatically, ignoring his overwrought warning.

'Okay. Be it on your own head then,' Kennedy replies in a resigned tone.

'So?' I prompt him, eager with anticipation.

Kennedy makes a sucking noise with his lips and slowly shakes his head, weighing the gravity of what he's about to reveal. 'Ruby was a mob patsy. But not in the way you think; the mob had nothing to do with my assassination,' he adds quickly, wanting to make the point crystal clear. 'As I told you, Oswald acted alone, period. Nonetheless, the mob quickly spotted an opportunity. They were desperate to get the government off their back, especially with Bobby's relentless crusade against organised crime breathing down their necks. On the night of the assassination, Giancana and Roselli saw a once-in-a-lifetime opportunity and took it – these guys were not shy. Their plan was audacious,' he snorts.

'They wanted to make the highest echelons of the US government believe they were not beyond the reach of organised crime: if they pushed too hard, they could be "got at" just like any other mob target. The mob knew suspicion would fall on them for my assassination, given the Cuban connections and Bobby's drive against racketeering. They wanted to give this suspicion enough credence to exert a "cautionary effect" on the government – you know, the "if they can get to Kennedy, then they can get to any of us" sort of paranoia, that would make crusaders like Bobby, or anyone else, back off in fear of their own safety.

'But it was a fine balancing act; to encourage a sense of conspiracy around mob involvement, but not so much that it would attract the full attention of the police and Feds. Roselli was well connected, very well connected, across the country and hit on the idea of using Ruby as a patsy. He was perfect in many ways; his mob connections were tenuous enough that no firm linkages could ever be proven but still implicit enough that many would assume the mob put him up to it. So, as their thinking went, if the mob ordered Oswald's killing, it could only be for one reason: to ensure Oswald never revealed the role of the mob in my assassination. And in some ways, they succeeded, didn't they? Here we are, sixty years later, still speculating about mob involvement in my assassination,' he says, shaking his head.

I'm finding it hard to process what I'm hearing. It's outlandish to be frank. Kennedy has not only debunked once and for all the multitude of conspiracy theories out there by confirming that Lee Harvey Oswald was the sole actor behind his assassination but has also exposed a hitherto unknown Mafia side plot that would make Machiavelli blush! But as I'm processing all this, one thing still doesn't add up, and that's again Jack Ruby. I turn to face the President.

'Why would Ruby agree to what was in effect a suicide mission? He gunned down Oswald in the full glare of the international media and with a dozen police officers standing by. This was only ever going to end in one outcome for him,' I state.

'Ruby was motivated,' Kennedy says, raising his eyebrows for emphasis. 'Roselli threatened to kill Ruby's wife, and she meant a lot to him – despite his unfaithfulness to her,' he adds. 'And of course, there was also the promise to put pressure on the DA, and even the trial judge, to secure a lenient outcome – the mob could do that in those days. And besides, Ruby had terminal cancer – no one apart from him knew that at the time.'

This story's got more layers than a Russian doll, I think to myself! And why hasn't any of this come to light before? Did it die with Ruby in prison in '66 and with the subsequent murders of Roselli and Giancana a few years later? As for Kennedy knowing all of this, I can only assume he's somehow seen "the files."

I mull all of this over, feeling awed by the revelations. But then again, apart from personal curiosity satisfied, what benefit can this information serve? No one's going to believe me. There's no evidence, save the fleeting words of a ghost and besides, would anyone even care nearly sixty years later? I'd just be another Kennedy conspiracy theory "nut job," albeit one late to the party.

These thoughts are suddenly interrupted. I can't say where it came from. I only hear the muffled bang of what I assume is a gun discharging. There's a hot, searing pain in my chest. I look up at Kennedy, my mouth agape, shock and disbelief etched on my face no doubt. He stares at me calmly, with steely eyes. As the lights go out and my brain fogs with confusion, the only thing I can hear are his words ringing in my ears, those words I so flippantly dismissed a few minutes earlier: "If I tell you, they'll kill you."

The End.

GLOSSARY

A Conversation With God

Arthur Dent – The protagonist of The Hitchhiker's Guide to the Galaxy, often referenced in discussions about the meaning of life.

Cretaceous-Paleogene event – A mass extinction event 66 million years ago, likely caused by an asteroid impact, that wiped out most species including the dinosaurs.

Dolós – In Greek mythology, the spirit of trickery and guile, often associated with deception.

Gavrilo Princip – The Bosnian Serb nationalist who assassinated Archduke Franz Ferdinand in 1914, triggering World War I.

Genesis – The first book of the Bible, which includes the creation story and the tale of Adam and Eve.

Janus – A Roman god depicted with two faces, symbolizing transitions, beginnings, and duality.

Milankovitch cycles – Long-term variations in Earth's orbit and tilt that influence climate patterns, including ice ages.

Mithras – A deity from the Roman mystery religion Mithraism, often associated with bull-slaying rituals.

Moses – A prophet in Abrahamic religions who led the Israelites out of Egypt and received the Ten Commandments.

Original sin – A Christian doctrine stating that humanity

inherits a sinful nature due to Adam and Eve's disobedience.

Zeus – The king of the gods in Greek mythology, often associated with thunder and lightning.

A Conversation With Gaius Julius Caesar

Actium – The site of the decisive naval battle in 31 BC where Octavian defeated Mark Antony and Cleopatra.

Alesia – The Gallic stronghold where Caesar achieved a major victory over Vercingetorix in 52 BC.

Artemidorus of Knidos – A philosopher who attempted to warn Caesar of the assassination plot with a written scroll.

Bithynia - An ancient region in northwestern Asia Minor, bordered by the Sea of Marmara and the Black Sea, which became a Roman Province after 74 BC.

Campus Martius – A large public area in ancient Rome used for military training, assemblies, and ceremonies.

Cassius Longinus – A leading Roman senator and one of the principal conspirators in the assassination of Julius Caesar.

Catullus – A Roman poet known for his scandalous and satirical verses, some of which targeted Caesar.

Cleopatra VII – The last active ruler of the Ptolemaic Kingdom of Egypt and Caesar's lover.

Curia of Pompey – The temporary meeting place of the Roman Senate and the site of Caesar's assassination.

Curule chair – A ceremonial Roman seat used by magistrates and high-ranking officials.

Decimus Brutus – A trusted ally of Caesar who ultimately betrayed him and joined the assassination plot.

Gaius Trebonius – A Roman politician and conspirator who helped isolate Mark Antony during Caesar's assassination.

Ides of March – March 15th in the Roman calendar, the date of Caesar's assassination in 44 BC.

Lupercalia – An ancient Roman festival of fertility and purification held in mid-February.

Mamurra – Caesar's chief engineer during the Gallic Wars, rumoured to be his lover.

Marcus Junius Brutus – A Roman senator and close associate of Caesar who ultimately joined the assassination plot, symbolizing betrayal.

Miletus – An ancient Greek city in Asia Minor, the target of a Roman campaign for which Caesar was sent to requisition ships.

Mithridates VI of Pontus – King of Pontus and long-time adversary of Rome, known for his resistance to Roman expansion.

Nicomedes IV of Bithynia – King of Bithynia, rumoured to have had a scandalous relationship with young Caesar.

Octavius (Augustus) – Caesar's adopted heir who became the first Roman Emperor.

Parthian Empire – A powerful empire in ancient Iran, targeted by Caesar for a major military campaign before his death.

Pharnaces – Son of Mithridates VI of Pontus.

Pompey (Gnaeus Pompeius Magnus) – Roman general and Caesar's political rival during the late Republic.

Pontus – A kingdom on the Black Sea coast, ruled by Mithridates VI, a major adversary of Rome.

Ptolemy XIII – Cleopatra's brother and co-ruler, who presented Caesar with Pompey's severed head.

Rubicon – A river in northern Italy famously crossed by Caesar, symbolizing a point of no return.

Thermus (Marcus Minucius Thermus) – Roman commander under whom Caesar served early in his career, known for reprimanding him after his extended stay in Bithynia.

Thirteenth Legion – Caesar's most loyal and experienced legion, crucial in his military campaigns.

A Conversation with Constantine XI Dragas Paleologos

Acciaioli, Nerio II – Florentine Duke of Athens and vassal of the Ottoman Sultan, forced to pay tribute by Constantine.

Adrianople – Modern-day Edirne in Turkey; served as an Ottoman capital before Constantinople.

Albania Veneta – Coastal territories in modern-day Albania that were under Venetian control.

Anatolia – A large peninsula in Western Asia that constitutes the majority of modern-day Turkey; lost to the Byzantines after the Battle of Manzikert.

Andronikos – Half-brother of Constantine XI.

Asia Minor – Historical term for the westernmost protrusion

of Asia, comprising most of modern-day Turkey.

Augusteum – A public square in Constantinople near the Hagia Sophia and the imperial palace.

Barbaro, Nicolò – Venetian surgeon and chronicler who witnessed the fall of Constantinople.

Black Sea – A large inland sea bordered by Eastern Europe and Western Asia, crucial for trade and military strategy.

Bosphorus – A narrow, natural strait and internationally significant waterway in northwestern Turkey that forms part of the continental boundary between Europe and Asia.

Boukoleon – The Palace of the Caesars in Constantinople, entered by Mehmed II after the conquest.

Campofregoso, Pietro di – Ruler of Genoa, personal enemy of the Doge of Venice.

Chalkokondyles, Laonikos – Byzantine chronicler.

Council of Florence (1431) – Ecumenical council where the union of Eastern and Western Churches was discussed.

Council of Ten – Governing body of the Venetian Republic.

Dardanelles – A narrow strait in northwestern Turkey connecting the Aegean Sea to the Sea of Marmara.

Demetrious – Nephew of Constantine XI, later betrayed him and became Admiral of the Ottoman fleet.

Despotate of the Morea – Byzantine territory in southern Greece ruled by Constantine before becoming Emperor.

Doge Francesco Foscari – Leader of Venice during the

events leading up to the fall of Constantinople.

Galata – A district of Constantinople across the Golden Horn, historically home to Genoese merchants.

Giustiniani, Giovanni – Genoese commander who led the defense of Constantinople's land walls.

Golden Horn – Natural harbour in Constantinople, where Genoese ships were docked.

Halil Pasha – Vizier of Mehmed II.

Hexamilion Wall – Defensive wall in the Morea, breached by the Ottomans in 1444.

Holy Wisdom, Church of the (Hagia Sophia) – Major cathedral in Constantinople, desecrated during the conquest.

Janissaries – Elite Ottoman infantry, central to the final assault on Constantinople.

Kerkoporta – A small postern gate in Constantinople, left open and exploited by the Ottomans.

Laetentur Caeli – Decree of union between the Eastern and Western Churches.

Lemnos – An island in the northern part of the Aegean Sea, also a Venetian possession.

Loukas Notaras – Megas Doux (Grand Duke) of Byzantium, opposed union with the Catholic Church.

Manzikert, Battle of (1071) – Decisive battle where the Byzantines were defeated by the Seljuk Turks, seen as the beginning of the Empire's end.

Marmara, Sea of – The inland sea connecting the Black Sea to the Aegean via the Bosphorus and Dardanelles.

Mesoteichion – Middle section of Constantinople's land walls, breached during the final assault.

Michael – Nephew of Constantine XI, betrayed him and became Governor of the Balkans.

Negroponte – The medieval name for the island of Euboea, a Venetian possession in the Aegean Sea.

Nicene-Constantinopolitan Creed – Statement of Christian faith debated during the East-West Schism.

Romanos IV Diogenes – Byzantine Emperor captured at Manzikert, ancestor of Constantine XI.

Rumelihisarı and Anadoluhisarı – Ottoman fortresses on the Bosporus.

Thessaloniki – City in Greece whose fall to the Ottomans alarmed Venice.

Vizier – High-ranking political advisor in the Ottoman Empire.

A Conversation with Albert Einstein

Adrianople – A historic city in modern-day Turkey, formerly an Ottoman capital, now known as Edirne.

Annus Mirabilis papers – Four groundbreaking papers published by Einstein in 1905 that revolutionized modern physics.

Asymmetric key cryptography – A method of encrypting data using a pair of keys (public and private) that is foundational to modern digital security.

British Museum (Rosetta Stone) – The Rosetta Stone, housed in the British Museum, was key to deciphering Egyptian hieroglyphs due to its trilingual inscriptions.

Cryptography – The science of encoding and decoding information to protect data from unauthorized access, widely used in military, financial, and digital communications.

Einstein–Szilárd letter – A 1939 letter from Einstein and Szilárd to President Roosevelt warning of Nazi atomic ambitions.

Frederick Lindemann – British physicist and scientific advisor to Winston Churchill who played a key role in wartime scientific policy.

Freud, Sigmund – Austrian neurologist and founder of psychoanalysis who corresponded with Einstein on the psychology of war.

General Theory of Relativity – Einstein's 1915 theory describing gravity as the curvature of spacetime caused by mass and energy.

Heinkel and Hellmuth Walter – German engineers who pioneered early rocket and jet propulsion technologies during WWII.

Komet (Messerschmitt Me 163) – A German rocket-powered fighter aircraft developed during WWII with limited operational success.

Loop Quantum Gravity – A modern theory attempting to unify general relativity and quantum mechanics by quantizing spacetime.

Manhattan Project – The secret U.S. project during WWII that developed the first atomic bombs.

Marie Winteler – Einstein's early romantic interest before his marriage to Mileva Marić.

Mileva Marić – Einstein's first wife and fellow physicist, with whom he had three children.

Newton, Isaac – English physicist and mathematician whose laws of motion and gravity laid the foundation for classical mechanics.

Oswald Mosley – British fascist leader in the 1930s who admired aspects of Nazi ideology.

Quantum computing – A field of computing based on quantum mechanics that enables exponentially faster processing for certain tasks compared to classical computers.

Quantum entanglement – A quantum phenomenon where two particles remain connected such that the state of one instantly affects the other.

Quantum teleportation – A process by which quantum information is transmitted between entangled particles, demonstrated experimentally with photons and atoms.

Rosetta Stone – An ancient Egyptian artifact inscribed in three scripts that enabled the deciphering of hieroglyphs.

Sigmund Freud and Einstein correspondence – A 1932 exchange titled "Why War?" discussing the roots of violence and human aggression.

Special Theory of Relativity – Einstein's 1905 theory stating that the laws of physics are the same for all non-accelerating observers and that light speed is constant.

Szilárd, Leo – Hungarian-American physicist who co-authored the Einstein–Szilárd letter and contributed to nuclear chain reaction theory.

V-2 Rocket – The world's first long-range guided ballistic missile, developed by Nazi Germany during WWII.

Wernher von Braun – German rocket engineer who developed the V-2 and later led NASA's Saturn V program.

A Conversation with William Shakespeare

Anne Hathaway – William Shakespeare's wife, whom he married

in 1582; they had three children together.

Christopher Marlowe – An English playwright and contemporary of Shakespeare, known for works like Doctor Faustus and The Jew of Malta.

Doctor Balthasar – The male disguise adopted by Portia in The Merchant of Venice to argue in court and save Antonio.

Doges of Venice – The elected leaders of the Republic of Venice, serving as heads of state from the 8th to 18th centuries.

Francis Bacon – An English philosopher and statesman, also proposed by some as a possible author of Shakespeare's plays.

Grammar school in Stratford – Likely refers to the King's New School in Stratford-upon-Avon, where Shakespeare is believed to have been educated.

Henley Street – The street in Stratford-upon-Avon where William Shakespeare was born and raised.

La Serenissima – A title meaning "The Most Serene Republic," used to refer to the Republic of Venice.

Lord Chamberlain's Men – A playing company for whom Shakespeare wrote for most of his career; later became the King's Men.

Oberon and Titania – The king and queen of the fairies in Shakespeare's A Midsummer Night's Dream.

Plutarch – Ancient Greek biographer whose Lives were translated by Thomas North and used by Shakespeare as a source for his Roman plays.

Portia (Doctor Balthasar) – A character in The Merchant of Venice who disguises herself as a male lawyer to save Antonio.

Sir William Stanley, 6th Earl of Derby – Another candidate proposed by some as the true author of Shakespeare's works.

The Castell on the Hoop – A tavern in Southwark, London, known to have existed in the Elizabethan era and frequented by actors and writers.

The Taming of the Shrew – A Shakespearean comedy about the courtship of a headstrong woman and her suitor, Petruchio.

Titus Andronicus – One of Shakespeare's earliest and most violent tragedies, set in ancient Rome.

A Conversation with Leonardo Da Vinci

Agostino Barbarigo – Doge of Venice from 1486 to 1501, known for his efforts to defend the Republic against Ottoman threats.

Andrea del Verrocchio – Renowned Florentine painter and sculptor who was Leonardo da Vinci's teacher and mentor.

Battle of Cascina – An unfinished fresco by Michelangelo intended for the Palazzo Vecchio, depicting a Florentine military victory.

Battle of Novara (1500) – A battle in which French forces defeated Ludovico Sforza, leading to his capture and imprisonment.

Bernardo Baroncelli – One of the conspirators in the Pazzi Conspiracy against the Medici family.

Bernardo di Niccolò Machiavelli – Father of Niccolò Machiavelli, a Florentine lawyer and minor nobleman.

Duomo (Florence Cathedral) – The cathedral of Florence, formally known as Santa Maria del Fiore, and site of the Pazzi Conspiracy attack.

Francesco Salviati – Archbishop of Pisa and co-conspirator in the Pazzi Conspiracy.

Francesco de' Pazzi – Member of the Pazzi family and a principal conspirator in the 1478 plot to assassinate the Medici brothers.

Il Principe (The Prince) – A political treatise by Niccolò Machiavelli, offering pragmatic advice on power and statecraft.

Michelangelo Buonarroti – Renaissance sculptor, painter, and rival of Leonardo da Vinci, known for works like David and the Sistine Chapel ceiling.

Palazzo della Signoria (Palazzo Vecchio) – Florence's town hall and the site of political power during the Renaissance.

Poliziano (Angelo Ambrogini) – Italian poet and scholar who was close to Lorenzo de' Medici and present during the Pazzi Conspiracy.

Reisläufer – Swiss mercenary infantrymen known for their discipline and effectiveness in Renaissance warfare.

Santissima Annunziata – A prominent church and monastery in Florence where Leonardo briefly stayed and worked.

The Battle of Anghiari – A lost Leonardo da Vinci mural depicting a Florentine military victory, commissioned for the Palazzo Vecchio.

The Hall of Five Hundred – The main chamber of the Palazzo Vecchio, intended to be decorated by both Leonardo and Michelangelo.

The Tamburo – A public letterbox in Florence used for anonymous accusations, often abused for political or personal vendettas.

The Virgin and Child with Saint Anne and Saint John the Baptist – A cartoon drawing by Leonardo da Vinci, admired for its composition and emotional depth.

A Conversation with John F. Kennedy

Apollo 11 – The 1969 NASA mission that successfully landed the first humans on the Moon.

Bay of Pigs Invasion – A failed 1961 CIA-backed operation by Cuban exiles to overthrow Fidel Castro's government in Cuba.

Checkpoint Charlie – A crossing point between East and West Berlin during the Cold War, symbolizing the division between the Soviet and Western blocs.

Cuban Missile Crisis – A 1962 confrontation between the United States and the Soviet Union over Soviet ballistic missiles in Cuba.

Dwight D. Eisenhower – The 34th President of the United States who preceded John F. Kennedy.

Fidel Castro – The revolutionary leader of Cuba who established a communist government after the 1959 revolution.

Jack Ruby – The nightclub owner who shot and killed Lee Harvey Oswald, the alleged assassin of President Kennedy, in 1963.

Lyndon B. Johnson – The 36th President of the United States who succeeded Kennedy after his assassination.

Martin Luther King Jr. – A civil rights leader who advocated for nonviolent resistance and delivered the 'I Have a Dream' speech in 1963.

Nikita Khrushchev – The Premier of the Soviet Union during the Cuban Missile Crisis and early 1960s.

PT-109 – A patrol torpedo boat commanded by John F. Kennedy during World War II, which was sunk by a Japanese destroyer in 1943.

Peace Corps – A volunteer program established by Kennedy in 1961 to promote peace and friendship abroad.

Robert F. Kennedy – U.S. Attorney General during his brother John F. Kennedy's presidency and later a U.S. Senator.

Warren Commission – The official U.S. government investigation that concluded Lee Harvey Oswald acted alone in assassinating President Kennedy.

www.ingramcontent.com/pod-product-compliance
Lightning Source LLC
LaVergne TN
LVHW010617100826
845148LV00014B/3007

* 9 7 8 1 7 6 4 5 6 6 6 0 5 *